mw BB

SPECIAL MESSAGE TO READERS

This book is published by
THE ULVERSCROFT FOUNDATION
a registered charity in the U.K., No. 264873

The Foundation was established in 1974 to provide funds to help towards research, diagnosis and treatment of eye diseases. Below are a few examples of contributions made by THE ULVERSCROFT FOUNDATION:

A new Children's Assessment Unit
at Moorfield's Hospital, London.

•

Twin operating theatres at the
Western Ophthalmic Hospital, London.

•

The Frederick Thorpe Ulverscroft Chair of
Ophthalmology at the University of Leicester.

•

Eye Laser equipment to various eye hospitals.

If you would like to help further the work of the Foundation by making a donation or leaving a legacy, every contribution, no matter how small, is received with gratitude. Please write for details to:

**THE ULVERSCROFT FOUNDATION,
The Green, Bradgate Road, Anstey,
Leicester LE7 7FU. England
Telephone: (0533)364325**

BODIE: HANGTOWN

Vicious Jody Butler had the run of the territory where his powerful father was the law. However, when Jody blew a man's head away with a shotgun, the townspeople of Pine Ridge decided they'd had enough and hired a killer called Bodie. Major Butler hit Bodie with everything he had, but Bodie soaked it all up and came back for more . . .

Books by Neil Hunter
in the Linford Western Library:

BODIE:
TRACKDOWN
BLOODY BOUNTY
HIGH HELL
THE KILLING TRAIL

First published in Great Britain

First Linford Edition
published July 1994

Copyright © 1979 by Neil Hunter
All rights reserved

British Library CIP Data

Hunter, Neil
 Bodie the stalker no.5: Hangtown.
 —Large print ed.— Linford western library
 I. Title II. Series
 823.914 [F]

ISBN 0–7089–7582–8

Published by
F. A. Thorpe (Publishing) Ltd.
Anstey, Leicestershire

Set by Words & Graphics Ltd.
Anstey, Leicestershire
Printed and bound in Great Britain by
T. J. Press (Padstow) Ltd., Padstow, Cornwall

This book is printed on acid-free paper

NEIL HUNTER

BODIE: HANGTOWN

Complete and Unabridged

LINFORD
Leicester

1

"YOU want to say that again?" Jody Butler asked.

The man seated at the table pushed his glass of beer aside and raised his head. "Sure," he said. "Go to hell! That's what I said, cowboy, and you take it any damn way you want!"

An ugly laugh rose in Jody Butler's throat. "Maybe you ain't realised who I am, mister."

"I know who you are," the man replied. "But it don't bother me. I never was one to get excited over a name."

The flesh of Jody's face darkened with the rise of colour. He jerked a finger in the direction of the man at the table. "You hear what this son of a bitch said? To me!"

Jody's three companions, lounging against the saloon bar, nodded their agreement. One of them stepped forward, his small eyes glittering with menace. He was a stocky man with heavy shoulders and a brutal, pockmarked face.

"Kick the bastard out of the chair if you want it, Jody. Don't do to let these assholes talk back. Only thing they know is a rap in the mouth."

"Yeah!" Jody grinned, sure of himself now that Haddon had backed him. "You going to make a choice, mister? Hard or easy?"

The man remained silent. Jody took this as a sign of defeat and glanced at Haddon, his grin widening. He was still grinning when the man at the table rose to his feet, grabbing up the chair he'd been using and swung it in a brutal arc. There was a sodden smack as the edge of the chair clouted Jody across the side of his face. He fell back, clutching a hand to the gash in his cheek, yelling in fright as he felt blood spurt through his fingers. There was a momentary confusion in Jody's mind, clouded by the pain swelling up in his face. Wild, uncontrolled anger rose and he snatched at the gun holstered in his right hip.

"Go ahead, boy, because I'd purely love to blow a hole right through your belly!"

Jody checked his right hand, blinking away the tears of pain misting his eyes. He looked in the direction of the man who had hit him, and saw that the chair had been exchanged for a double-barrelled shot gun. The muzzles were aimed directly at Jody. He stared down the black bores and a sick feeling crawled over him. Jody jerked his hand away from his gun as if the weapon had become red hot.

"Now keep still," the man with the shotgun said. "All of you! It's time somebody told you people how this town feels. We've had to put up with you damn cowmen for too long. Comin' down out of the hills with your herds. Driving them here to Pine Ridge 'cause we've got the railroad. We put up with that. This is cattle country. But we don't see why we have to put up with your people walkin' all over our town like it was yours to treat how you like. This is our home — not some place where you can raise hell and pay no mind to the mess you leave behind. Ain't right we should have to step aside for you. Or give up somethin' just 'cause you want it. You want to act like pigs — then go home and do it! But don't bring your dirt to Pine Ridge and foul the streets!"

"Mister, the Major ain't goin' to be too happy when he gets to hear how you treated us," Haddon said.

"You can tell the Major that Nate Gower couldn't care less how he feels. You tell him to run his town the way he wants, but in Pine Ridge he's just another cowman."

"Damn you!" Jody Butler screamed. "My father could buy this town ten times over!"

"Dare say he could," Gower said.

"But owning a town ain't all there is to it. Town's no more than wood and nails and glass. It's people who matter — an' there ain't money enough in the world can buy you those!"

"Bull!" Jody raged. "You'll see, Gower! It ain't over yet! I'll fix you!"

"Right now," Gower pointed out, "the best thing you can do is get out of here. Find the doc and get him to patch you up 'fore you bleed to death!"

Jody Butler suddenly remembered his gashed face. He turned pallid white, his flesh greasy with sweat. He threw a glance in Haddon's direction.

"Let's get out of here," Haddon growled. He jerked a thumb at the other two men. They moved to help the softly moaning Jody Butler across the saloon and out of the door.

There was a strained silence in the saloon, broken when the bartender picked up a washed glass and began to wipe it dry. "Thought I was going to need the sawdust there for a minute, Nate," he said.

Nate Gower lowered his shotgun. He stepped up to the bar, releasing a long-held breath. "That was close as I ever want to get! Give me a whisky, Vic."

The bartender filled a glass. "On the house," he said. "That's been a long time coming, Nate, and needed saying."

Nate Gower drained the glass, shuddering as the whisky burned its way down to his stomach. "Son of a bitch," he said softly.

The bartender raised his eyes. "Jody Butler? Yeah. They should've drowned him at birth! Ain't nothing but pure meanness all the way through. Nate — you keep your eyes skinned. That Butler kid — he could take it in his mind to hurt you. Not the sort to be happy at getting pushed around himself."

Gower nodded. "I was thinking the same myself, Vic." He grinned, none too convincingly. "I'll be all right." He picked up the shotgun. "This'll make sure!"

He had convinced himself that the matter was ended a few hours later. He completed his business in town, and towards the latter end of the afternoon was on his way to the livery stable to pick up his horse for the ride back to his ranch. His mind was absorbed with other things, mainly concerned with the fact that he had secured a loan from the bank which would enable him to build the new barn he needed.

So he didn't notice the shadowed figures lurking in the mouth of an alley he was drawing level with. Or the man who moved up behind him, something gleaming coldly in his right hand. There was an instant when Gower became aware of the man behind him and he began to turn, his face taut with alarm. He was too late. Something smashed brutally against the side of his skull. Pain exploded inside his head. Numbing, blinding pain. Gower uttered a stunned cry. He felt his limbs weaken. There was a sick feeling rising in his stomach. He lurched drunkenly. Then hands reached out and caught hold of him and he was dragged into the dusty alley. He was flung to the ground, hitting the rough earth hard, his mouth scraping against something sharp. Blood spurted from a gashed lip. Gower lay in semi-darkness, dazed, unsure of what was happening. It had all been too fast.

"Well now, look what happened to Mister Gower!"

The voice was unmistakable even to Gower. He would have recognised the taunting tones of Jody Butler anywhere.

"He don't look so tough to me," said Lee Haddon. He drove the toe of his heavy boot into Gower's ribs. "Hell, listen to the bastard moan!"

Jody Butler, leaning against the side of the building that formed one wall of the alley, fingered the bandage on his cheek. "Get him to his feet!"

Still half-dazed, spitting blood from his mouth, Nate Gower felt himself being hauled upright. He peered through glazed eyes at the leering faces before him.

"Come on, Gower," Jody Butler jeered. "Don't go falling asleep on us. This is all for your benefit. Wouldn't want you to miss all the fun!"

"You want first go?" Haddon asked.

Jody giggled softly. "No, Lee, I'll let you have him. You got the touch."

"Yeah!" Lee Haddon said, and then he began to hit Gower. He worked steadily, methodically, his gloved fists brutally working back and forth across Gower's face and body. His blows were delivered with the maximum force to create the most painful results. After a couple of minutes he stepped back to survey his handiwork. He was sweating, his pockmarked face streaked.

"I bet you thought we'd forgot about you, huh?" Jody Butler sneered. "I said I'd get you, Gower, an' I mean what I say! You figure you hurt now — well just wait until we're through!"

One of the two men holding Gower upright reached and took a handful of the rancher's hair, yanking his head up. Jody Butler almost yelled out with pleasure when he saw what Haddon's fists had done to Gower's face. There was hardly a square inch of flesh left unmarked. Gower's face was a mass of bruised, gashed bloodiness. His nose was crushed almost flat. The left eye was covered by a sticky spread of blood from a cruel gash angling down across the cheek. There was a raw, pulpy mess where his mouth had been, the lacerated lips having been smashed back against the teeth again and again until flesh and gums and broken bone had become almost one.

"He's finished, Jody," Lee Haddon said. He had peeled off his bloodstained gloves and was lighting a thin Mexican-made cigar he had shipped up from Nogales. "Ain't no good punchin' away at a man who can't feel it."

"I don't figure to let him off on account he ain't awake!" Jody screamed. He whirled around and spotted Gower's shotgun lying in the dirt. Bending he snatched up the weapon and dogged back both hammers. "Hey, boys, you reckon this'll make him sit up and take notice?"

"Hell, Jody, take it easy!" Haddon yelled.

Jody's face grew taut, the reckless streak in him taking control of his emotions.

"You growin' a yellow streak, Lee?" he challenged.

"You know better than that," Haddon said. "Far as I'm concerned you can cut him in half! But you shoot off that scattergun and the whole damn town's going to be on our backs!"

"Who cares about a horseshit place like this," Jody screamed. His eyes were wide and staring, his whole body stiff with tension. And he had already committed himself to the act he now carried through.

The narrow alley was filled with the shattering blast of the exploding shotgun. A cloud of powdersmoke momentarily obscured the figure of

Nate Gower. He was still being held upright by Jody Butler's men — but as the smoke cleared it was to reveal that they were supporting a headless corpse. Jody had thrust the shotgun close up to Gower's face and pulled the trigger. The devastating power of point-blank discharge had literally blown Gower's head of his shoulders in a hideous explosion of shredded flesh and bone, hair and blood. Bits of raw flesh and brains spattered the wall behind Gower's body. A gout of blood fountained up from the pulped neck where Gower's head had been only a second before. The decapitated corpse jerked and kicked, as if life still existed — which it did for a short time — until the escaping rush of blood starved the heart and it ceased to work. Raw nerve ends transmitted their final spasms and Nate Gower became nothing more than a dead weight in the arms of the men holding him.

"Judas priest," one of them said. "That weren't funny, Jody! You might of hit Travis or me with that scattergun!"

"You ever known me to miss what I aim at?" Jody asked, grinning. "Hell, Brenner, a blind man couldn't have missed that shot!"

"Never mind the talk," Haddon said. "We don't get out of here, Gower's goin' to have company!"

"Damn right," Brenner agreed. He nodded to Travis and they both released their hold on Gower's corpse, letting it flop to the ground.

The four men ran to the mouth of the alley, bursting out on to the street. Their horses were standing at a hitch rail on the far side of the street.

"Come on," Haddon yelled.

They were halfway across when men started to appear, running down the street towards them.

"See what you've done now, Jody?" Travis grumbled. "Aw hell boy, I could kick your goddamn ass for pullin' a fool stunt like that!"

Jody grinned. He turned abruptly, bringing up the shotgun and triggered off the second barrel in the direction of the advancing crowd. A man went down in the dust, clutching hands to a bloody thigh.

"That's enough, Jody!" Lee Haddon warned.

"Go screw yourself," Jody whooped. He yanked out his revolver and started to shoot.

"Son of a bitch!" Haddon growled. He pulled his own gun and slugged Jody behind the ear.

Brenner and Travis had the horses free by this time and they turned to help Haddon. He let them take Jody's limp form. Bending he picked up Jody's gun, using it and his own to lay a volley of well-placed shots at the feet of the oncoming crowd, scattering them. Jody had been dumped across his saddle, and as Haddon mounted his own horse he took the dangling reins of Jody's mount in his left hand.

"Go!" Haddon screamed. "Go!"

The horses thundered off towards the outskirts of town, a desultory peppering of shots following in their wake. Thick dust rose from beneath the pounding hooves, concealing them from the guns of the outraged citizens of Pine Ridge.

They left behind them an angry town, one man wounded and another one very dead. Though it might not have been of much concern to anyone at the time, they also disturbed the sleep of a man in one of the front rooms, on the second floor of the Pine Ridge Cattleman's and Businessmen's Hotel.

The man, who was not alone in his bed, was not a cattleman, or a businessman in the strict sense of the word. If he had to be classed he would have been labelled as a specialist. A specialist in an anti-social profession. He was a hunter. A hunter of men — men outside the law — men who had outraged and violated society — men who carried a price on their heads. Once an upholder of the law himself and now simply an extension of the system, he worked according to the letter of the law — which allowed him the freedom to hunt down and, if the need arose, to kill the lawbreakers. He was a bounty hunter.

His name was Bodie.

2

"PLEASE sit down, Mister Bodie," the grey haired man said.

Bodie sank into one of the comfortable leather armchairs, taking a quick look round the expensively furnished office belonging to Lew Masters, the president of the Pine Ridge Bank.

"Can I offer you anything, Mister Bodie?" Masters asked. "A drink? Cigar?"

Bodie shoot his head. "I'll settle for an explanation," he said.

A nervous smile touched Master's lips. He wasn't sure yet how he should treat this man. But he was realising fast that Bodie had no time for fripperies.

"Very well. Let me introduce my fellow council members." Masters indicated the fat, bald headed man on his left. "Orville Prine. And this is Jonas Wayland," he went on, lifting a hand in the direction of the stern, cold eyed man seated on his right.

"I guess this has something to do with the upset yesterday afternoon?"

Masters nodded. "Not the kind of incident we wish to encourage in Pine Ridge, Mister Bodie."

"We intend to stamp out such lawlessness," Jonas Wayland stated. Bodie glanced in his direction. One look at the man and Bodie knew Wayland was one of the old school. He was a straight-down-the-line man. There wouldn't be any deviation from his single minded dealings with lawbreakers. Given the opportunity Wayland would have hung every transgressor he got his hands on. "Pine Ridge is an expanding community. We are attracting investors and people all the time. The last thing this town needs is an epidemic of violence and killing."

"You'd prefer a quick trial and a good, clean hanging," Bodie said, his eyes fixed on Wayland's face.

To his credit Wayland never even flinched. "Just that," he snapped. "We want Jody Butler and the other men involved in the killing of Nate Gower brought back to Pine Ridge to stand trial. And if they are found guilty, then they'll hang! Do you see anything wrong in that, Mister Bodie?"

"No. Tell me, Mister Wayland, are you going to put the rope round their necks personally?"

Lew Masters gave a muffled cough and Orville Prine raised his eyes to the ceiling, desperately trying to find something to look at.

Only Jonas Wayland remained unmoved. He leaned back in his seat and for a brief moment Bodie was sure he caught the makings of a thin smile on his lips.

"Let me put it this way, Mister Bodie. If the need arose I certainly wouldn't back down."

I'll bet you wouldn't, Bodie thought. He turned his attention back to Lew Masters.

"You putting out a bounty on these men?" he asked.

Masters nodded quickly. "We are prepared to offer 15,000 dollars for the capture of the four men involved in the killing of Nate Gower and the wounding of Ben Halstead." He picked up a printed poster and handed it to Bodie. "These will be officially displayed, of course, as the law demands, but . . ."

Wayland grunted impatiently at Masters's hesitation. "What Lew is trying to say in his polite way, Mister Bodie, is that we would prefer you to deal with the matter. Your reputation is known even this far north, and if we want this job done properly then it is common sense to go to the best man." He smiled frostily. "It's to our advantage that you happened to be in Pine Ridge at this time."

Bodie looked up from reading the poster. "Is there anything special about this Jody Butler?" he asked.

"He's the only son of Howard

Butler," Wayland explained. "And Howard Butler is the wealthiest and most powerful cattleman in the area. He runs a spread large enough to be classed as a small country. He even has his own town, and he rules with a heavy hand. In his own territory he's the law, the judge, and the jury."

"Almost a man after your own heart," Bodie murmured.

"I'll admit the man has qualities I admire," Wayland said. "But they are overshadowed by his faults. Butler rules by fear. By the threat and use of violence. He will not tolerate any kind of challenge to his right to run things the way he does. He's hard and tough and he doesn't even understand the meaning of the word compromise. It's his way or nothing."

"I take it that the boy — Jody — tends to play on his father's name?"

"Precisely," Orville Prine said, opening his mouth for the first time. "He treats everyone and everything with equal contempt. As if he has the right to do whatever he wants, take whatever he wants."

"Let's call it by the right name," Wayland said. "Jody Butler is a mean, vicious little bastard who only walks tall in his father's shadow. As far as I'm concerned he's gone beyond the limit this time. Killing Nate Gower was a bad mistake. There's no way Jody Butler can buy himself out of this damn mess."

"The Major will do his best to do just that," Lew Masters said.

"The Major?" Bodie glanced at him.

"Oh yes," Masters said. "Howard Butler did army service during the war. He kept his title even after he'd been discharged. Everyone calls him the Major."

Bodie folded up the wanted poster and tucked it in his coat. He picked up his hat from the floor beside his chair and climbed to his feet.

"Been a pleasure meeting you, gentlemen," he said.

Lew Masters looked faintly surprised.

"I . . . er . . . does this mean you'll be taking up our offer?"

Bodie smiled. "Let's say I'm thinking it over. Good morning, gentleman."

As the door closed behind the tall figure of the dark suited manhunter, Lew Masters leaned back in his seat, releasing a pent up sigh.

"That man scared the hell out of me," he admitted. "I had the feeling he could have cut my throat without even raising a sweat."

"What did you expect?" Jonas Wayland asked sharply. "The man is a bounty hunter, not a preacher. He puts his life on the line every time he goes after someone. Living under that kind of pressure is bound to affect a man's personality."

"An unpredictable personality," Orville Prine said.

Wayland smiled. "But just the right man to stand up to someone like the Major."

"I wonder if Bodie realises the kind of man the Major is?" Masters asked.

"What he'll be up against if he does decide to go after Jody Butler?"

"He'll handle whatever comes his way," Wayland said.

"You talk as if you're sure he'll take the offer."

"He'd decided before he left this room," Wayland assured the banker.

"You know something we don't," Jonas?" Orville Prine inquired.

Wayland's eyes glittered. "I know men like Bodie, Orville. Hand him an opportunity to go after someone like Jody Butler and he'll walk through hell to see it through!" He nodded at some inner thought. "Do some checking on Bodie's background — you'll see what I mean."

Wayland stood up and gestured in the direction of the tray of drinks on Masters's desk. "Now how about that drink, Lew!"

★ ★ ★

Drink was the last thing on Bodie's mind. On leaving the bank he made his way across the street to the town jail and went inside. Pine Ridge's lawman was a long faced individual named Butterick. He was lounging back in his swivel chair reading a dog-eared magazine, and he did little more than raise his eyes as Bodie entered the office.

"Made it official have they?" he asked.

Bodie helped himself to a cup of coffee. He crossed the office to where a large map of the territory was pinned to the wall. For a while he studied the map.

"I hear tell this feller called the Major is some kind of big fish in his own pond," he said.

Butterick tossed his magazine on the desk. "Long as he stays in that pond I don't give a damn."

"What's the set up in this town he runs?"

"Elkhorn is pretty much Butler's town all right. If he don't own it outright he's got money in most of the businesses. Same with the folk. They work for him or owe him. Not all, and them as do don't like it, but they ain't got much say in the matter."

"There any law?"

Butterick smiled indulgently. "The kind you'll like, Bodie," he said. "The marshal is Butler's man all the way. Daren't blow his nose without the Major's say so."

"He got a name?"

"Frank Lowery. Now I ain't one for handin' out advice, Bodie, but I'll say this once. Don't trust that son of a bitch one inch! If he tells you the sky's blue — you go outside and check for yourself!"

"What kind of a ride is it to Elkhorn?"

"Close on three days," Butterick said. "Pretty high country up there. Trails are thin. Man riding to Elkhorn would tend to cut his own."

Bodie traced the route on the map.

"You figurin' on maybe catchin' up with those boys 'fore they reach

Elkhorn?" Butterick asked.

"Could save a lot of trouble," Bodie said. "I'd sooner face four than take on Butler's whole crew."

* * *

Bodie returned to the hotel and made his way up to his room. He went in, closing the door and tossing his hat on the bed. There was a slow stirring beneath the covers and a tousled blonde head appeared, blue eyes gazing sleepily around the room.

"Lord, what time is it, Bodie?"

Bodie answered by drawing back the curtains. Bright sunlight streamed into the room. The girl in the bed groaned as if she was in mortal pain, dragging the covers over her face.

"Bodie, you're a sadist! How could you do a thing like that to a girl! Jesus, I wouldn't be surprised if I'm scarred for life!"

"Don't get in a panic, honey, it's only the sun. Didn't you know folk actually walk around in it and it gets so they like it. You ought to try it sometime."

As he walked by the bed Bodie reached out and caught hold of the covers, dragging them off the girl, leaving her naked on the crumpled sheet.

"Have a heart, Bodie," she grumbled. "I ain't used to being exposed to the daylight. I only function properly in the dark."

Bodie grinned. "So I noticed last night," he said.

The blonde rolled lazily on to her side and lay watching Bodie pack his gear into his saddlebags. After a while she got off the bed and padded across the floor to him.

"Hey, you leaving, Bodie?"

"Yeah."

"It's going to be dull around here," the girl said. She leaned her firm body against him, thrusting her full breasts against his back.

"You'll survive," Bodie said.

"Sure," the girl sighed. "Hey, where're you going, Bodie?"

"Hunting!"

"I thought you found what you were lookin' for last night."

Bodie slipped his arm round the girl's slim waist, easing her round to face him. "That's right," he said. "It was just where you said it'd be." He slid his hand down her warm body, feeling her pliant flesh shiver. "Still there too!"

The girl squirmed expectantly, long thighs parting in anticipation. "Bodie, you ain't in a hurry to leave are you?" she asked.

"Let's say I ain't in so much of a hurry I can't say goodbye."

The girl drew him down on to the bed, smiling eagerly. "I always did prefer saying goodbye like this. Much nicer than just shakin' hands, don't you think, Bodie?"

"Honey, from where I am, whatever it is you're shakin', it's a safe bet hands ain't even in it!"

3

"THE Major's goin' to raise the roof over this mess," Brenner said over the rim of his coffee cup.

Lee Haddon stretched his legs out, poking at the ashes of the small fire with the heel of one boot. "So you keep sayin'. What the hell do you want me to do? Bring Nate Gower back to life?"

"What the Major wants to do is to put that little shit on a goddam lead!" Brenner said savagely. "Hell, Lee, ain't nobody likes to kick up a bit of hell better than me. But that damn kid is crazy. He's liable to turn round and shoot one of us if the notion strikes him."

Haddon glanced out beyond their camp. They had chosen a spot close to the edge of one of the wide, placid lakes that were often to be found in this high country. Ringed by the ever-present rise of the ascending peaks and bordered by thick stands of timber and grassy meadows, the lakes lay deep and silent, the undisturbed surfaces reflecting the surrounding land. They were a thing of beauty in a land of savage grandeur to anyone with the time to pause and take a long look.

"Where is he now?" Haddon asked.

Brenner shrugged, indicating that he also didn't really care where Jody Butler was. "He ate breakfast and then upped and wandered off."

"He's probably pulling wings off flies," Haddon muttered. He picked up the frying pan and scooped out the last slice of bacon.

"Lee," Brenner said.

"What?"

Brenner scratched his chin. "Why ain't they come after us?" he asked, voicing the question they'd all been asking themselves. "What the hell they playin' at back in Pine Ridge?"

Haddon wiped grease off his mouth with the back of his hand. "Wish I knew. But I don't figure to hang around until they do make up their minds. So let's break camp and ride."

While Haddon and Brenner started to gather their gear Travis rode in. He'd been back down their trail a way, checking to see if there was sign of any pursuit.

"Anything?" Haddon asked.

Travis swung down off his horse and helped himself to the last of the coffee. "Nothin'," he grunted. "It don't sit right, Lee."

"We just been sayin' the same," Brenner told him.

"Yeah, well it ain't doin' us any good jawin' about it, so let's move," Haddon said.

"Where's Jody?" Travis asked.

"I hope he's fell in the goddam lake and drowned," Brenner snapped.

"If it wasn't for the fact he's the Major's kid I'd push the bastard in myself," Haddon said. "But if we let anything happen to him the Major's going to make us damn sorry. And I ain't about to upset the Major."

"Well, next time we got to push some beef to market we leave Jody back at the spread. Major or no Major, I didn't sign on to wet-nurse a lamebrain like Jody Butler!"

"The Major wouldn't like to hear you talkin' like that, Brenner," said Jody Butler. He had come up on them unnoticed, out of the brush. He stood watching them, a faintly mocking grin curving his mouth.

"The Major ain't here, sonny, Brenner said. "And don't you try holding him over my head, you little asshole! You got us into this mess of trouble 'cause beatin' the shit out of that feller Gower just weren't enough for you! The big Jody Butler had to go and kill him! Boy, I hope your daddy whips the skin off your ass!"

Jody's grin widened for an instant, then faded. He stared hard at Brenner, shifting his gaze when Brenner refused to back down. "Go to hell," he muttered savagely and stamped off to his horse.

"All right," Haddon rasped. "We'll talk later. The best thing we can do now is get some distance between us and Pine Ridge."

They threw the remaining gear on their horses and mounted up. Without further delay they cut off around the perimeter of the lake, making for the high-rising green slopes on the far side. There was little to be said between the four — each had his own thoughts on the situation and its possible outcome. They were hard men, born and bred to the harshness of the land — yet they were as conscious as any to the rough justice liable to be meted out to the transgressors of the fragile peace existing in this untamed land.

Close on noon they halted for the first time to rest the horses. For the past couple of hours they had been climbing steadily, much of the time through densely wooded slopes. With the sun blazing down from a clear sky both men and horses were sweating and weary.

Lee Haddon eased himself stiffly from his saddle. He cuffed back his stained hat, flicking beads of sweat from his face. "Goddamn country," he growled. "Boils a man dry in summer and come winter she'll freeze your ass off soon as think about it!"

Brenner chuckled. "And on top of all that you got to ride herd on the Major's kid! Hell, Lee, it's real tough at the top!"

Haddon's grim expression did little to improve his looks. "You want the job?" he asked.

"Me?" Brenner shook his head. "No. I'm happy pushin' beef around."

"Yeah? Well you just . . . !" Haddon's voice faded away to silence as he found himself staring at the horseman who had emerged from the thick stand of timber only yards from where they had halted.

The rider had a levelled and cocked

rifle in his hands and a hard gleam in his eyes, and Haddon, cursing inwardly, knew that they had been taken. For one wild moment he was tempted to go for his gun, but caution overrode his reckless impulse — he knew damn well that if he pulled his gun he'd be a dead man. Lee Haddon was a lot of things, though a fool was not among them. He had no desire to die for nothing. And he had no intention of dying on account of Jody Butler.

4

"THE guns on the ground," Bodie said evenly. "Handguns first. Then the rifles. And don't be fooled by my good manners. First one who does anything to make me nervous is going to get himself very dead!"

The guns were tossed to the ground. Bodie edged his horse forward until it was standing over the pile of weapons. He wedged the butt of his rifle against his hip so he had a hand free to pull out the folded wanted poster he'd brought from Pine Ridge.

"They rate you fellers pretty high back in Pine Ridge," he said, shaking the poster open. "Paying a fat bounty. And they prefer you alive. Seems they're arranging a special day for you."

Lee Haddon made an angry sound. He glared up at Bodie. "A goddamn bounty hunter! That's why they didn't come chasin' after us in a bunch! They hired this miserable son of a bitch to do their dirty work!"

"You upset about something, feller?" Bodie asked. "Still I reckon you got cause. Must be a mite unsettlin' knowing you're on your way to a hanging — more so 'cause it's your own!"

"A funny man!" Haddon spat. "Give me a chance, mister, an' I'll have you laughin' so hard it'll kill you!"

"Ain't no way you're takin' us back to Pine Ridge!" Jody Butler yelled. He waved a threatening finger at Bodie. "My father . . . !"

"Boy, you wave that finger at me again I'm liable to cut it off and shove it down your throat," Bodie warned. "And don't give me any bullshit about your old man. I don't scare easy, and one of the things that don't scare me at all is hearing about big men with big names. Now if you ain't got anything better to say I'd advise you to keep your mouth shut!"

"Mister, I hope you get the chance to meet the Major," Brenner said, grinning. "I somehow figure it'd be an interestin' day."

"I reckon I'll have to live without that," Bodie said. He jerked the muzzle of his rifle. "Time we moved. It's a long ride back to Pine Ridge so the sooner we start the sooner you boys can be relaxing in the town gaol."

Jody Butler let out a wild screech and rammed his spurs into his horse's sides. The startled animal bolted forward, colliding with Brenner's mount. Brenner, almost unseated, yanked on the reins and his horse lunged to the side. It twisted wildly, its rear end barely missing Bodie's horse. Bodie's horse stepped back, hooves striking the pile of guns on the ground, and it sidestepped hurriedly. There was a split second when Bodie's rifle moved off target, and Lee Haddon, watching intently, used that moment. He ducked low, under the neck of Bodie's horse, coming up on the manhunter's blind side. Reaching up Haddon caught hold of Bodie's gunbelt and dragged the manhunter out of the saddle.

As Bodie went down he lashed out with the Winchester. He felt the barrel crack down across Haddon's shoulder, but it was too late to stop him from falling. Bodie hit the ground partly on top of Haddon, felt the man roll under him. Haddon's hands reached out and took hold of the Winchester. Bodie drove a hard fist into Haddon's side, hearing the man grunt.

He sensed movement around him, and knew that the other men had joined in. Strong hands grabbed at his clothing, dragging him across the ground. Somebody tore the rifle from his hands. Bodie kicked out and felt his boot strike soft flesh. A man cried out and Bodie recognised Jody Butler's voice. Then a hard blow caught him across the side of the skull. Brutal punches rained down on him until his face and body throbbed with pain. He felt his body being dragged over so that he was lying face down, and then he became aware of the cold muzzle of a gun being pressed cruelly against the side of his face. The hammer went back with a deadly sound.

"Bastard!" Lee Haddon said. "Son of a bitch near broke my shoulder with that Winchester!"

"Kill him! Kill him!" Jody Butler shrieked.

"You crazy bastard!" Haddon roared. He spun on his heel and lashed out, his big fist catching Jody across the mouth. The force of the blow drove Jody backwards until his feet went from under him. He hit the ground and lay staring up at Haddon, blood dribbling from his torn lips.

"Now shut your mouth, Jody, and don't open it until I say so," Haddon said.

Brenner, who was kneeling beside Bodie, his gun held against the manhunter's face, grinned at Haddon. "Aw, I wished I could of done that!"

"So what do we do with this one?" Travis asked.

Haddon was silent for a time, and then he smiled grimly. "We send him back to Pine Ridge," he said. "Let 'em see it ain't about to do 'em any damn good sending people after us. Give 'em a warning. Make 'em think twice 'fore they go hirin' any more bounty hunters!"

"An' how do we warn 'em?" Travis asked.

Haddon closed a hand into a big, solid fist. "Get him on his feet an' I'll show you."

Travis moved to help Brenner and between them they hauled Bodie upright. There was a moment when Bodie might have broken away from them but Brenner rapped the muzzle of his gun against the manhunter's cheek.

"You could be dead, friend," Brenner pointed out, "so I wouldn't push your luck!"

Haddon moved round so that he was standing in front of Bodie. He flexed his hands inside the thick leather gloves, taking his time, sizing up Bodie's physical appearance. Only when he was satisfied did he make his first move. Even Bodie, who knew what was coming, reacted too late. Haddon's right fist drove deeply into his stomach, hurting despite the taut stomach muscles. The force of the blow rocked Bodie back on his heels, only the restraining hands of Travis and Brenner keeping him on his feet.

"Hey!" Brenner said eagerly. "You want to make a bet on how long he lasts?"

Travis grinned. "This is one hard son of a bitch! He's liable to outlast Lee!"

"Yeah?" Haddon said peevishly, seeming to take the remark personally, and slammed another hard fist into Bodie's stomach. "Don't hold your breath on that, Travis!" He was staring directly into Bodie's eyes as he spoke and the mocking expression he saw mirrored there only added to the anger he already felt.

There was a brutal savagery behind the punch Haddon sledged to Bodie's jaw. The blow landed with a sodden smack, the rough hide gloves Haddon was wearing tearing the flesh, opening a raw welt that glistened with blood. Bodie's head snapped to the side, his vision blurring, the inside of his skull seeming to come apart. He didn't even see the next punch. It caught him full in the mouth, mashing his lips back against his teeth. Blood washed down his throat making him choke. The beating began in earnest then, Haddon using the same technique he'd employed on Nate Gower. But there was a difference this time — a cold, unfeeling yet deliberate intent to inflict pain, to hurt and to mark — though not so much that the victim might die. It was an ugly act of pure brutality.

For Bodie it became a drawn out episode when time and events merged into a meaningless blur. After the first few minutes pain as such meant nothing to him. He wasn't even certain if he was conscious or not. His senses were dulled from the ceaseless pounding of Haddon's fists against his face and body — a relentless barrage that went on and on with the eternal rhythm of waves battering a rocky shore. There were brief flashes of lucidity when Haddon's bitter, sweating face rose out of the mist drifting across Bodie's eyes. Then during another clear moment he saw that the face had changed — this time it was Brenner, then Travis, and later Haddon again — each of them taking a turn, each of them smashing blow after blow. And every now and then the pain would surge up out of the dull ache spreading over his body — blinding, silent explosions of pure agony like white hot spears driving deep into his very being.

It went on and Bodie had no way of knowing how or when it stopped. His first full awareness of feeling above the pain allowed him the sensation of a gentle rocking movement. A steady to and fro motion. Bodie struggled to open his eyes but they were too badly swollen and caked with congealed blood to allow him more than thin slits. He looked out on a dazzling splash of green that was laid against a sharper blue. He couldn't understand what it was at first, and then he figured he must have been seeing the lush foliage of trees framed against the sky. Then the colours drifted away as his pain ridden body refused to accept responsibility for the hurt any longer, and shut down. A darkness that was deeper than any night invaded his mind, accompanied by a silence that was frightening in its intensity . . .

First he was cold . . . it was a bone-deep, nagging cold and it dragged Bodie up out of the darkness . . . shivering . . . awareness brought a resurgence of pain that threatened to tear him apart. Bodie stirred sluggishly, his tortured senses unwilling to respond at anything more than minimum efficiency. It took Bodie a long time to realise he was sitting saddle on the back of a horse, and even longer to understand that he was tied in the saddle. A rope looped around each leg had passed beneath the horse's belly. Another length of rope secured his hands to the saddlehorn. He made a token effort to free himself but the action proved too much for him and he drifted off again . . . he came out of it the next time to find the cold even worse. Peering out through his slitted eyelids he caught a glimpse of bright stars in the night sky . . . from the high mountain peaks a raw wind fingered its way down through the timbered slopes, clawing at his bruised and bloody face . . . Bodie lifted his head, sucking in a lungful of the crisp air in an attempt to clear the savage pounding from his skull . . . the resultant pain dragged a ragged moan from his lips . . . he slumped in the saddle, sweat beading his face . . . chest heaving with gulping sobs as he tried to catch his breath . . . almost afraid to breath in case the pain returned . . . he knew that one or more of his ribs must have been cracked, the others badly bruised.

Judas Priest, he thought, the bastards really worked me over! Yet in the same instant he acknowledged that they had done him a favour — and it was that they had left him alive! Barely alive — but still, that was their mistake. A bad one on their part. He had suffered at their hands and he'd go through a hell of a lot more before he recovered . . . but recover he would. He wouldn't allow them the same option when the time came for an accounting. A cold, almost inhuman smile curved up the corners of Bodie's battered mouth. The smile cost him dearly but he ignored the pain. Pine Ridge could forget its hanging party. Bodie would deliver the wanted men . . . but this time he would do it his way and be damned to the rest of them. The day he brought back the fugitives they wouldn't arrive in any other position than face down over their saddles!

But that was something for the future. Bodie had more pressing problems at the moment, and his main concern was getting himself free of the ropes holding him in the saddle. It took him a long time. Most of the rest of the long, dark night as his horse patiently plodded on through the darkness. Dawn was starting to grey the sky again when Bodie finally slid his hands free from the bloodied coils of rope. The flesh of his wrists lay burned and raw from the constant twisting and pulling. The first thing Bodie did was to gather up the loose reins and pull the horse to stop. He leaned over and fumbled with leaden fingers at the rope around one ankle. Once he had it loose he kicked the rope free from his other leg, grinning crookedly with relief. The grin lasted just the length of time it took for him to slip from the saddle to the ground. He hit hard, twisting on to his back, struggling to get up and knew no more . . .

Warm sunlight on his face . . . the distant sound of a bird in some high treetop . . . closer, the steady crunch of his horse chewing on thick grass . . . he moved slowly, stiffness making his movements clumsy as he sat up. He lifted his hands to his swollen face, carefully touching the lumpy, blood-caked mask. He felt grotesque. Every feature was twice its proper size. Lips thick and split . . . one side of his nose puffed up . . . cheeks bulging like some bloated, nightmarish creature . . . eyes still half closed . . . and blood everywhere, dried and blackened, clinging to the raw edges of the gashes that marked the swollen flesh.

Bodie climbed to his feet and walked with hesitant steps to where his horse stood. The animal raised its head as he shuffled closer, regarding him with stolid indifference. He caught hold of the saddlehorn with one hand, using the other to free the canteen of water hanging there. Uncapping it he lifted the canteen to his mouth and allowed the cool liquid to trickle down his throat. The simple act of swallowing made him wince. As he hung the canteen back on the saddle he noticed that the saddlebags on his side of the horse were unstrapped. He lifted the flap and saw that his gunbelt and holstered Colt had been jammed into the pouch. Bodie dragged the belt out. Even his knife was still in its sheath. He held the belt in his hands, staring at it, then shrugged and looped it round his waist. He took out the Colt and checked that it was fully loaded. On an impulse he moved round to the other side of the horse. His Winchester was in its scabbard. He couldn't figure that all out right there and then. First they beat him half to death, tie him on his horse and send him off, but before they do they return his weapons! Bodie didn't dwell on the matter too much at that point. The effort of just thinking seemed to be too much for him.

"All right, feller," he told himself. "You got off the damn horse without any trouble. Let's see you get back on!"

He practically dragged himself back

on the horse an inch at a time. By the time he slipped his feet into the stirrups he was drenched in sweat, his body trembling from the effort. He gathered up the reins in his right hand. His left arm was held against his body, pressuring over the damaged ribs in an attempt to reduce the pain. Jabbing in his heels he turned the horse in the direction of Pine Ridge. It lay over half a day's ride away. Like it or not, Bodie admitted that he was going to need help. He wasn't of any use to himself at the moment, let alone the people who were expecting him to bring in the killers of Nate Gower. First off he needed experienced medical care. The sooner he got it the better — because then he could start to mend, and that couldn't be soon enough for Bodie. He had a job to finish. Up to now he'd made a mess of the whole affair, and those four bastards were probably well on their way to Elkhorn figuring they'd scared off any possible pursuit. Well maybe they had — for the time being. Sooner or later, though, Bodie was going to be well enough to pick up the trail again. And then Elkhorn was going to experience a hard time, and so would anyone who happened to get in the stalker's way.

5

HOWARD BUTLER — the Major — looped the reins of his big chestnut around the smooth hitch rail and stepped up on to the verandah of the Elkhorn Palace Hotel. He paused before entering the lobby, taking time to look out over the town, deliberately letting himself be seen. It was an imperial gesture, one that fitted Butler's self-imposed superiority. He enjoyed the moment, savouring the knowledge that amongst those on the street who could see him, there were a fair number who disliked him — even hated him. That knowledge did nothing to spoil Butler's moment. If anything it helped to add a certain spice. The fact that he was disliked wasn't going to bother him because there was no way any of those people could touch him. He was too powerful.

Too wealthy. And he held the town of Elkhorn in the palm of his hand.

A moment later he strode into the hotel, his polished boots sinking into the thick lobby carpet. Butler took off his hat, smoothing a big hand across his thick hair. He crossed the lobby, nodding briskly in the direction of the fawning clerk behind the desk. He went through an arched entrance that led directly to the hotel's private lounge bar. It was a long, low room, the walls panelled with rich dark wood. The furniture was heavy and comfortable. Butler glanced around the room. He caught the eye of the man behind the bar and raised a finger. The barman nodded and began to prepare a drink. Butler walked the length of the room, heading for a corner where three men were seated around a table. They had drinks in front of them and a blue haze of cigar smoke hung over their heads.

"Talking about me, boys?" Butler asked coldly as he moved round the table and took his place in the fourth chair.

"No," one of them said bluntly. He was a solid, big framed man in his early fifties, his thinning hair silver grey. Blue eyes regarded Butler steadily. There was little love lost between the two men. Miles Frazee, the town's banker, was one of the few influential men Butler had been unable to buy. They disliked each other personally yet business drew them together. "Actually we were just ironing out a few points about this railroad deal."

Howard Butler's interest sharpened. He leaned forward in his chair. "You've heard something?"

"Negotiations are much further advanced than at our last meeting," Frazee said.

"Good!" Butler hesitated for a moment. Then: "Well? Do I have to drag it out of you word by word?"

"The situation as of this moment is that the railroad will agree to running in a spurline to Elkhorn, providing that we can guarantee access to all the surveyed land between the main line and the town's limits."

"Excellent," Butler smiled. He waited impatiently as the barman approached the table with a thick tumbler of brandy. When the man had gone Butler took the glass and tasted the contents. Surveying the silent faces before him he placed the glass on the table's green baize surface. "Something's wrong? Come on then. Let me hear it."

On his left the slight figure of Peter Stern shifted uncomfortably. He ran the local land agent's office, a firm of which Butler was a major stockholder.

"Is this something that concerns you, Stern?"

Stern's pale face took on a sickly hue and he refused to look at Butler. It was Frazee who spoke.

"There has been a setback, Howard," he said — he was the only man in town who had the nerve to use Butler's given name. He knew it angered Butler.

That was the main reason he did it. "A number of the smaller outfits along Kittyhawk Creek have formed an alliance to oppose the railroad coming through. They maintain that the spurline will cut directly across their range. Ruin their livelihood. Peter has made them generous offers for their land — but they won't sell."

Butler's face darkened with rage. "God damn it, they have to sell! Don't they realise the benefits this spurline will bring to Elkhorn? The money? The increased investment?"

"They don't see it that way, Major," Peter Stern blurted out. "As far as they are concerned all it means is that they lose the land they've owned for a long time."

"With the money they'll get they can buy better range elsewhere," Butler snapped.

"I think you'll have a hard time convincing them of that, Howard," Frazee said. "The Kittyhawk range is good country. You'd have to go a long way to find such ideal conditions. And most of those outfits have been there for a very long time. Amos Skellhorn's owned his land for over twenty years."

"Skellhorn! Damn that man," Butler rasped. "I'll wager he's the one who thought up this so-called alliance. He only has to snap his fingers to have every man on Kittyhawk Creek dancing his tune!"

"Must be frightening to have such a hold over people," Frazee murmured dryly.

Butler glared at the banker but held his tongue. He turned his attention to the fourth member of the group. Randolph Meers was a lawyer. He was Howard Butler's lawyer. Which meant he was a very busy man.

"Nothing to add, Randolph?" Butler asked.

Meers shook his head. He was a round shouldered, thin man who wore a permanently gloomy expression on his sallow face. "I have checked the ownership of the land in question in depth. Every legality is sound. I'm afraid there isn't a thing we can do in that respect, Major."

Butler sat back in his seat, drumming the fingers of one hand on the edge of the table. The others watched him, waiting, knowing that the problem was in his hands now.

"All right," Butler said. "It seems I'll have to try my way."

He stood abruptly, snatching up his hat, and with a curt nod he strode out of the room. On the verandah he stopped long enough to put his hat on, then crossed the street and made his way to the long, low granite building that was Elkhorn's gaol. Pushing open the door he went inside, his boots rapping loudly on the hard wood floor.

The office was spacious and well-furnished by comparison with the majority of law establishments. It should have been because Butler had spent a lot of money on the place. He also spent a fair amount on the man who ran the gaol — Frank Lowery. He'd picked the man up in Laramie three years ago. Lowery had been a deputy then. He enjoyed the power that went with wearing a badge and he was just the man Butler had been looking for. Lowery had a weakness — he liked money and he was easily bought. Butler brought him to Elkhorn and used his influence with the town council to get Lowery appointed as marshal. It was as easy as that. And it meant that Butler had his man just where he wanted him.

"Frank? You in?" Butler called. He strode down the length of the office, impatience clouding his face. "Frank!" There was a sound from the back of the gaol, where Lowery had his living quarters. Moments later Lowery appeared in the doorway, buttoning his shirt. His face was flushed, his thick hair untidy.

"Caught you with your pants down, did I, Frank?" Butler asked, a sly grin on his lips. He was aware of Lowery's other vice. Young girls were to Lowery what liquor was to other men — he couldn't leave them alone, nor could he ever have his fill.

"I was . . . er . . . just gettin' tidied up," Lowery mumbled. He scraped his fingers through his tangled hair, smoothing it down as he hurried round to sit behind his expansive desk. He cleared his throat. "Morning, Major."

Butler settled himself into a seat, resting his hat on his knees. "Frank, we have a slight problem," he said, and outlined the difficulties being created by the ranchers on Kittyhawk Creek.

"Skellhorn!" Lowery said. "He's always been a damn troublemaker." He stroked his lower lip. "Can he really foul up the railroad deal, Major?"

"Damn right he can! But I don't intend to let him, Frank. There's too much at stake here to allow any interference. That spurline can make Elkhorn's future. No doubt about it, Frank, the railroad's going to be the major lifeline of this country. So we need it here in Elkhorn, and by God we're going to get it!"

Lowery's lean face flushed with excitement. "Maybe we can do something about Skellhorn and his alliance, Major," he said. "Something like a late night call from a few community-minded citizens!"

Butler smiled. "That should make an impression on Skellhorn. Shake him up a little. Put the fear of God in the whole of Kittyhawk Creek!"

"Leave it to me, Major," Lowery said. "I'll arrange a visit for tonight. By the time the boys have finished, Skellhorn's going to think the sky's fallen in on him!"

Butler left the office, satisfied that he had things moving nicely. He made his way back to where he'd left his horse. He was just freeing the reins when a shadow fell across him. Glancing up he recognised Lee Haddon looking down at him from the back of his horse.

"What you doing in town, Lee?"

Haddon cuffed his hat to the back of

his head. "Looking for you, Major," he said. "We got troubles."

Butler climbed into the saddle and motioned for Haddon to ride alongside of him as they left town. "So?"

"It's Jody," Haddon told him.

Butler sighed. "I figured as much. What's he up to now?"

"He's sayin' he ain't staying up on the canyon any longer, Major. Not even for you. Major, it's hard on the boys having to put up with his bad mouthin' 'em all day."

"Goddam that miserable . . . " Butler caught himself. He threw a hard look at Haddon. "We'll ride back to the ranch and then I'll come up to the canyon with you. Jody's going to stay right there until I tell him to come down. He'll do it if I have to beat the hide off him." A look of regret crossed his face. "Maybe that's what I should have done years back, Lee. Instead I indulged him. I gave him too much money and too much freedom, and look what it's made of him."

"Hell, Major, it ain't your fault," Haddon said. "A man's either got the making in him or he ain't. Jody — well, beggin' your pardon, Major, he just ain't got what it takes."

"Anyway, Lee, I'm grateful for what you and the boys have done. Getting him out of Pine Ridge and sending that bounty hunter packing. That was loyalty I won't forget."

"Hell of a thing to have happened in the first place," Haddon admitted. "Beating up on that feller Gower would have been enough — but Jody turnin' round and blowing him apart just caught us on the hop."

"It was a stupid thing to do," Butler said. "No justification at all. That's why Jody has to stay out of sight until time goes by and I can see what I can do."

They left Elkhorn far behind, curving off into the dense wooded slopes of the mountains, following the well-defined trail that led directly to Butler's vast range. Soon they were crossing wide grassy meadows dotted with huge herds of contented cattle, each wearing the Circle-B brand. The home ranch lay an hour's ride from town, on the extreme edge of Butler's range.

The ranch complex was a huge affair, almost a small village, with its numerous buildings and corals. There was a cluster of small huts belonging to married members of Butler's staff. The bunkhouse itself could house close on forty men. There were huge feed barns, great stables, a wagon shed. There was a well-equipped blacksmith's forge as well as a carpenter shop, where the skilled craftsmen had the capacity to make anything in wood, from a simple chair all the way up to a complete wagon. The main house was the central feature of the place. Though only two storeys high it had spread over a large area, since the original structure had been extended and added to over the years. It was built of local stone, masterfully blended with wood, and stood as a monument to the achievements of the man who owned it. Like the house, Butler himself was solid and unmovable, capable of withstanding any storm, resistant to change, unbending, unyielding.

"Lee, give me half an hour, then we'll take a ride up to the canyon and settle this matter with Jody," Butler said as he dismounted before the house.

Haddon nodded. He took the reins of Butler's horse and led it off to the stable to be looked after by the old Mexican who had been with the Major right from the start.

Butler went inside the house. He tossed his hat on a chair, unbuttoning his coat as he crossed the polished wooden floor of the spacious living-room. He poured himself a drink and went to stand in front of the wide fireplace. On the wall over the fireplace hung a large oil-painting. The picture was of a young and beautiful girl. Butler raised his eyes and studied the painting, all the old memories flooding back. It happened every time he looked at the image of his late wife. Twelve years she'd been dead now and he missed her more with each passing day. The painting had been his wedding present to her. She had been nineteen when they had married, and she had died on her forty-sixth birthday. Jody had been their only child, coming late, and while Butler's wife had been alive she had doted on the boy. Butler himself had contributed towards this, mainly because it made his wife happy — and her happiness meant everything to him. Her death turned life sour. There was a vast, aching emptiness he had to fill, so he plunged himself even deeper into increasing his power, his property, because it was the only thing left for him.

He quickly found out Jody's inability to turn his hand to anything except cards and whisky and girls. Butler masked his disappointment and devoted himself to full-time involvement with his spread. He knew now that he'd been wrong. Giving Jody his freedom, money, the time to indulge himself, had been the wrong way. The fact was proven out now — with Jody killing someone — and no matter how he felt about his son he was determined to get him out of this mess one way or another. Whether Jody liked it or not!

6

"WHEN are you leaving?" Jonas Wayland asked.

"In about an hour," Bodie said. "Less if you stop asking your damn fool questions!"

Wayland ignored the jibe. "Doctor Fullerton tells me he won't be responsible for any setbacks. Apparently you hurt his feelings when you suggested an alternative place for keeping his stethoscope."

Bodie thumbed in the final bullet and snapped the loading gate shut, spinning the Colt's cylinder. He jammed the gun into his holster and hooked the hammer loop in place.

"I've already wasted ten days," he snapped. "Damned if I'm going to waste any more."

"It isn't going to be easy getting close to Jody Butler this time,"

Wayland pointed out.

Bodie managed a cold smile. "You mean last time was easy?" He touched his fingers to the still-healing bruises on his face. "I'd swear I got these somewhere!"

"What I was trying to point out, Bodie, is that Jody Butler will have the protection of his father's not inconsiderable crew. And every man the Major employs has to be as good with a gun as he is with a trailherd — if not better."

"Wayland, I know what you're getting at," Bodie said. "But it ain't going to make any difference this time how many folk Jody Butler has round him. I figure to bring him in. I made a mistake last time round and I paid for it. But one thing about me, Wayland, is that I never make the same mistake a second time. I learn each time I do something wrong. What I learned this time was hammered home pretty deep. It means that the next time I put my eyes on Jody Butler or any of those bastards who were with him I put them down fast. No talk. No fuss."

"I hope that doesn't mean you intend to bring Jody Butler back dead, Bodie!"

"Mister it means I don't intend to give that little pissant one thin chance. And if that's going to upset your hanging party — well hard luck on you. If I bring him back dead, Wayland, I figure you'll hang him anyway, just for the pure hell of it!"

Wayland scowled at the thought. "Likely I will at that," he snapped.

Bodie picked up his gear, tucking his Winchester under one arm. He opened the door of his room. "Fixin' to stay, Mister Wayland?"

Wayland strode past him. Bodie closed the door and followed the man downstairs. At the desk Bodie handed over his key.

"Your horse is outside, Mister Bodie. Saddled and ready," the desk clerk told him.

Bodie fastened on his saddlebags

and jammed his rifle in the scabbard. He checked the saddle-girth before he mounted up. Wayland was standing on the edge of the boardwalk, a bleak look in his eyes.

"Something stuck in your craw, Wayland?" Bodie asked.

"I was just thinking about the injustice you'll do this town by bringing Jody Butler back already dead!"

Bodie squared the brim of his hat down over his eyes. "Tough, Wayland, but it's gone beyond just being another bounty. Right now I aim to bring Jody Butler in for my own reasons. Your damn town and its hanging fever just got shoved down to second place. Be seeing you, Mister Wayland, and you can count on that!"

He left the town behind him, following roughly the same route he'd taken before. For the first couple of hours his stiff body refused to accept the discomfort of a hard saddle, but later Bodie found he was adjusting to being up and about again. He knew he'd been right to quit Pine Ridge. He had spent over a week putting up with the doctor's petty restrictions, done nothing but rest. The first few days he hadn't argued — but soon after, once his body got over the initial shock of the savage beating, Bodie got that restless urge. He took to exercising a little each day. Never mind what the damn doctor said, he'd thought, I ain't just sittin' like some ninety-year-old and going stiff all over! By the end of the first week most of the swellings had gone. His face and body were still discoloured with bruises but Bodie was not about to go in for any beauty contests. He allowed himself one concession to the doctor's advice and left on the tight bandage binding his torso. The doctor had checked him over and found that no ribs were actually broken, as Bodie had thought they were. They were badly bruised and maybe one had a slight crack. All the doctor had been able to do was strap them up tight and wait for Nature to effect its cure. Bodie figured that by now Nature had had her chance, and he couldn't hang on any longer.

He rode steadily, trailing up through the lower slopes of the Tetons, cutting through timberline and out on to the high grass meadows, with the sheer peaks looming ahead of him all the time, framed against the sharp-bright, crystal mountain air. He rode across lush arenas of knee deep, sweet grass, skirted bottomless, placid lakes. He saw wild game in abundance and every stream and creek was thick with darting fish. He saw it all, and not for the first time did he try to figure out why men had to kill each other over land like this. There was plenty and enough for them all — but his own question provided its own answer. Man, by his very nature, was a greedy son of a bitch, and he only had to take a look at something good to want it all for himself. He was never satisfied with a little. He had to take, and grab, and if he saw his neighbour had a slice just a little juicier, then he naturally had to reach out and take that too. Which led to the inevitable conflict.

Bodie took three days to reach Elkhorn. During the trip he ate well and got plenty of rest. He figured now was the time for these things — because once he got to Elkhorn he might find himself on the busy side.

Mid-morning on the fourth day he was in the timbered hills above the town. He'd settled his horse out of sight, taken his rifle, and perched himself where he could watch the town without being spotted himself. Not that there appeared to be all that much to see. Elkhorn looked pretty much like a dozen other towns Bodie had seen. It was neat and clean, its streets set out in regular lines. It had a church and a school and a bank. Indications of its well-established existence. This was no prairie-dog town. No grubby border village. Elkhorn was a prim and proper, white-painted, Sunday-go-to-meeting type town. Or so it seemed on the surface. But according to what

Bodie had heard it was a bought town. Paid for and run by one man with a lot of money and an equal amount of power.

Major Howard Butler!

The father of the man Bodie was looking for. Not that Butler's alleged power, his wealth, meant a deal to Bodie. He wanted Jody Butler and the men who had ridden with him from Pine Ridge. And he was going to get them all — one way or another!

Bodie stayed up on the hill for a couple of hours. By the time he moved he had Elkhorn's layout imprinted on his mind. He retrieved his horse and climbed into the saddle. He kept his rifle in his hand, resting it across the front of his saddle as he rode down out of the timber, picking up the trail that led into Elkhorn.

He entered at the south end of town, taking his horse up the dusty street as far as the Crystal Palace Saloon. Here he dismounted and tied his horse, keeping his rifle handy as he made his way inside the saloon. It was a large place, well-furnished and decorated. Behind the long bar were high shelves, all of them stacked with unopened bottles. Bodie made his way to the bar and signalled to one of the white-shirted bartenders.

"Beer," he said.

The bartender brought it and watched Bodie drain half the contents down his throat. He flicked imaginary dust from his shirt cuff.

"Don't recall seeing you in here before," he ventured.

Bodie peered at him across the top of the glass. "Can't say I recollect you, feller, but I ain't about to let it get the better of me."

The bartender laughed without too much conviction. "I only meant I didn't figure you worked for any of the outfits round here."

"That a rule before you can get a drink or something?"

The bartender frowned, not sure what he'd started, or how far it might go. He edged away from Bodie.

"Seeing as how you like talkin', feller, you can tell me something," Bodie said, catching hold of the bartender's white shirtsleeve. "Which way to the Butler spread?"

"The Major's?" the bartender queried.

"The one and only," Bodie agreed.

"Straight on out of town. Head north. There's a regular trail out to the place. You can't miss it."

Bodie nodded, letting go of the bartender. "Thanks."

He finished his beer and paid for it. Outside, on the saloon's verandah he looked for a place to eat and spotted a restaurant a little way up the street. Bodie untied his horse and led it towards the restaurant. He figured he might as well eat now. No telling where his next meal might be coming from, or when. It was an old rule but a good one — eat while you can because the next mealtime might be a long way off! The same rule applied to sleep. It could also be held true for something else,

Bodie thought, grinning to himself. Hell, there were times when a man could find himself pretty short on that too! He tied his horse to the hitching post and went inside the restaurant. A tall, boney girl with pale eyes and a too-wide mouth served him. Every time Bodie caught her eye, she grinned at him, smoothing her wrinkled dress down over her wide hips. Apart from that Bodie enjoyed the meal. It was well cooked and there was plenty of it. He finished off with two cups of black coffee. The gawky female brought his bill and took Bodie's money with a final grin. Bodie picked up his rifle and left the place. He closed the door behind him and turned towards his waiting horse — and walked right into three levelled, cocked guns.

"Ain't no need for those, fellers, I paid for the meal," Bodie said, taking in the sobering fact that each of the men had a bright silver badge pinned to his shirt.

"Smart mouths usually get rapped,"

the middle one said. He was tall. Young and rawboned. Thick, corn yellow hair hung down from his hat. He stared at Bodie with hooded blue eyes.

"Smack him in the mouth, Rick," one of the others urged. He was a runty little man with a brown, wrinkled face. He rubbed the back of his hand across his mouth in nervous anticipation.

The one called Rick blinked his hooded blue eyes. "Frank said to bring him in, Shorty, and that's what we do."

"We going somewhere, fellers?" Bodie asked.

"Marshal wants to see you," Rick said. "I'd advise you to come along and don't get smart. But first you hand over that rifle and the handgun."

Bodie did as he was told. Only a damn fool tried to outsmart three cocked and levelled guns, and anyhow he figured it would be worth a walk up the street to meet Elkhorn's lawman.

"Vinnie," Rick told the third man, "you bring his horse along."

They made their way along to the impressive town gaol. While the one called Vinnie saw to Bodie's horse, the other two escorted Bodie inside the gaol.

Elkhorn's marshal, Frank Lowery, glanced up as Bodie was brought in. He eyed the tall manhunter, realising that this man was no saddletramp. Lowery leaned back in his seat, watching Bodie carefully.

"You were asking questions about the Butler spread," Lowery said.

"There a law that says I shouldn't?"

"Mister, all you need to know is that I'm the law in Elkhorn, and when I decide something needs looking into we look into it!" Lowery's face tensed. "What's your interest in the Butler spread?"

"That's my business, Lowery, and unless you got a charge you can make stick I'm leaving!"

"The hell you are, mister!" Lowery yelled, half-rising from his seat. He jabbed a finger at Bodie. "I can toss you in a cell and forget about you if I want — and, mister, right now that's just what I want!"

"I said we should have smacked him in the mouth!" said Shorty.

"Too late, Shorty," grinned Rick, and without prior warning he lifted Bodie's rifle and clubbed him across the back of the skull with it. Bodie stumbled forward, pain blazing at the back of his eyes. He collided with the front of Lowery's desk and caught a glimpse of Lowery's brutal face leering at him. Bodie threw a wild swing at that face, but his timing was off and he missed. Then Rick clouted him a second time with the hard butt of the Winchester and the day went black. Bodie pitched forward, striking the desk and bouncing off on to the hard floor. He hit hard but he didn't feel a damn thing. The pain came much later . . .

7

HE had a terrible headache when he woke up. He was lying on a hard bunk, with only a thin mattress beneath him, and he knew damn well that he was in one of the cells at the rear of Elkhorn's gaol.

Bodie lay still. He couldn't be certain but he was sure someone was watching him through the bars, and he didn't want anyone to know he was awake. Out of the corner of his eye he was able to see out through the small barred window set high in the stone wall. The sky was rapidly darkening. That meant he'd been out for a good few hours. The deputy named Rick had really put some weight behind that clout, Bodie realised, and decided to remember that! Things weren't going too well for him at present. He'd hardly been in Elkhorn for more than a couple of hours and here he was locked up in the damn gaol! Maybe you're losing your touch, he told himself. First you get yourself beaten to a pulp and then get tossed in the pokey! Not exactly the way to convince yourself you've still got what it takes.

He heard a door open and close quietly not too far off. A man approached the cell.

"He awake yet?" It was Rick's voice.

"He ain't moved a muscle all the time I been watchin'." The second man was the one called Shorty. "Hell, Rick, maybe the son of a bitch is dead! You laid that rifle on him damned hard!"

"Balls!" Rick muttered softly. "He's got a thick skull."

"Well if he ain't awake by the time Frank gets back here with the Major we'll be likely finding out how thick yours is!"

"Yeah?" There was a pause — then: "Unlock that goddamn door, Shorty, I'll find out whether he's awake or not! Just keep your gun handy!"

A key rattled in the lock. Bodie heard the door creak as it was swung open, and he grinned wolfishly into the shadows as he heard Rick cross the stone floor of the cell. Just keep coming, you son of a bitch, Bodie begged. Come and see what I got for you! One way or the other something was going to be decided in the next few minutes. If that cell door was unlocked, then Bodie was going to do everything in his power to get out through it. Because he'd had his gutful of being knocked around and generally treated as if he was nothing more than a . . .

"The bastard's breathing anyhow!" Rick's voice came from just above Bodie, right alongside the bunk.

Bodie felt Rick's hand on his shoulder. The deputy began to roll Bodie away from the wall, turning him over on to his back so he could see Bodie's face. Bodie didn't resist. He let his body turn, waiting until he was facing Rick, and hoped that his legs hadn't got cramped from lying on the bunk for so long — because he was going to look a real idiot if he leapt up off the bunk and fell flat on his face.

"Well?" Shorty asked. "He awake or what?"

Damn right I'm awake — Bodie agreed silently, then dragged his right leg back and then forward, the heel of his boot smashing into Rick's stomach. The big deputy let out a strangled scream as raw pain exploded through his body. He was driven back across the cell, his arms waving uselessly as he tried to regain his balance. He saw Bodie's tall figure erupt off the bunk, coming at him in a wild lunge, and there wasn't a thing he could do to stop the man.

Bodie drove his left shoulder into Rick's chest. He could see the open cell door at Rick's back, and the other deputy — Shorty — halfway through, his gun waving about in his raised fist. Shorty couldn't fire because Rick was in the way and Bodie wanted the situation to stay that way for the time being. There was a moment when it seemed Shorty was going to get by Rick's stumbling figure. But then Rick slammed up against the cell's open door. His heavy body swung the door shut.

"Hey!" Shorty yelled as the solid frame of the iron door drove at him. His cry was cut off abruptly as the edge of the door hit him across the side of the face with a meaty thud. Blood poured from the long gash in his cheek, soaking the collar of his shirt. Shorty tried to drag himself back through the door and almost managed it — but Bodie, seeing the deputy's retreat, put his foot against the door and gave it a vicious shove. There was a crunch of breaking bone as Shorty's right arm was caught between door and frame. Shorty let out a shrill scream. The fingers of his hand opened in a spasm of pain and his gun clattered to the floor of the cell. Bodie twisted away from Rick's sagging figure. He scooped up the gun and turned back towards

Rick as the deputy took an uncertain step away from the cell door. Rick's face was ashen, his mouth hanging open as he tried to suck air into his lungs. He didn't even lift his hands to protect himself as Bodie stepped in close, swinging the gun in his hand like a club. The barrel slammed across Rick's skull — once, twice, then again. Rick went down like a felled tree — and Bodie was sure he felt the building shudder as he hit the stone floor. Reaching out Bodie yanked open the cell door. Shorty was clinging to one of the bars. His right arm hung limply at his side. The sleeve, from the elbow down, was sodden with blood and it was dripping from Shorty's fingers in a constant stream.

"You bastard," Shorty sobbed. "You broke it — you broke my goddamn arm — you bastard!"

Bodie tried to look sympathetic — even while he was sledging his fist across Shorty's jaw. The deputy rolled along the bars of the cell. Bodie had to hit him three times before he went down.

Bodie made his way along the passage leading to the front of the gaol. He checked that the office was empty before he stepped through. It took him a couple of minutes to locate his gunbelt and his rifle. Bodie strapped the belt on and checked the Colt. He did the same with the rifle, and then made for the door.

It opened before he reached it. Lowery's third deputy — the one called Vinnie — stepped into the office. He took one look at Bodie and began to yell, reaching for the gun on his hip.

Bodie was on him before the gun was even halfway out of the holster. His right fist caught Vinnie under the point of his jaw, the impact snapping Vinnie's head back and lifting his feet clear off the floor. Vinnie crabbed sideways along the wall, trying to regain his balance. Bodie swung a booted foot and knocked Vinnie's legs from beneath him. Vinnie bounced as he hit the floor, throwing out a hand to try and ward Bodie off. Bodie easily avoided the hand, lashing out with his foot again. The heel of his boot caught Vinnie in the head. There was a dull thud as Vinnie's skull rapped hard against the stone wall of the office, leaving a bloody stain behind.

Bodie turned towards the door and flung it open. He stepped outside. As he did a gun exploded behind him, the bullet ripping a white chunk of wood from the door frame. Bodie snatched out his Colt, twisting round. On the far side of the office, lurching out through the doorway leading to the cell block, was Rick. He was staggering drunkenly. Blood streaming down his face, soaking his shirt. But he had a gun in his fist and he was capable of using it. Bodie didn't hesitate. He snapped off a single shot, saw the bullet strike Rick in the chest. The impact of the heavy .45 bullet twisted Rick around, bouncing him off the wall. Bloody debris erupted from the pulpy hole in Rick's broad back as he slid down the wall and curled up in a wriggling heap on the blood-spattered floor.

The second he saw his bullet hit the target Bodie turned and ran across the street. He wanted to get as far as he could from the gaol before anyone else came out. By a lucky chance the street was deserted, this being the time in early evening when the stores had just closed and people were sitting down to the last meal of the day. Bodie knew his luck couldn't hold for too long. The sound of the shooting would bring the curious and the morbid out for a look — he wanted to be out of sight before that happened. He reached the shadows of the boardwalk on the far side of the street and moved steadily away from the gaol. In the distance he heard somebody yell and knew that the street would be filled with people very shortly. The best thing he could do was to dodge down the next alley.

He drew level with the restaurant

where he'd eaten earlier. It was in darkness. As Bodie stepped by the door it opened with a soft rattle and a tall figure revealed itself in the shadows.

"Quickly! Inside!" A slim female arm and hand reached out and tugged at his shirt, drawing Bodie inside the dark restaurant. The door closed, the dry sound of a bolt being snapped into place reaching Bodie's ears as he stood there, straining to see who had come to his aid. "Through to the back," came the voice. Nervous hands prodded him forward, across the gloomy restaurant, guiding him around the end of the counter and through the curtained doorway.

Warm, pleasant smells invaded Bodie's nostrils, and he realised he was standing in the kitchen. An oil lamp, suspended from the ceiling, threw out a faint light from its turned down wick.

Bodie saw the tall figure of the girl who had served his meal reach up and raise the flame of the lamp. Soft light flooded the kitchen. The girl turned to glance at him, the pale eyes a little frightened as she faced him. She unconsciously put a hand to her untidy hair, lifting stray curls away from her moist forehead. Almost guiltily she plucked at the open neck of her dress, covering the exposed flesh of her throat.

"You'll be safe here," she said.

"Maybe," Bodie said, unsure of her reasons for doing for him what she had. "I don't fancy the idea of getting myself boxed in."

The girl smiled — the expression was completely removed from the almost childish grin she had used earlier. "Trust me," she said. "They'll expect you to make a run for it. Not stay in town. Isn't that what you were planning?"

Bodie had to admit she was right. That had been his intention — to get as far away from Elkhorn as he possibly could. He stared at the girl, his mind working furiously. She had a point. About him staying in town. It was the least likely place for him to be, and being so close to the Elkhorn gaol might turn out to be the safest.

"I open up for the evening trade in an hour," the girl said. "Then I close at ten. There's a room upstairs you can use. Rest if you want to. The room overlooks the street so you can keep an eye on the gaol."

"You make it sound tempting," Bodie said.

"From the look of you a rest wouldn't do much harm." The girl stepped closer. "Is that blood over your ear?"

Bodie reached up and touched the place where Rick had clouted him with the Winchester. Dried blood had formed a brittle crust over the tender spot. "Compliments of Elkhorn's law!" he muttered.

"True to form," the girl snapped. "The shooting I heard? Was anyone hurt?"

"Deputy name of Rick," Bodie said, watching for the girl's reaction.

"Badly?"

"I put one where it hurts most," Bodie told her.

The girl didn't even flinch. "No more than he deserves," was all she said.

"That's pretty strong coming from a female," Bodie observed.

The girl had picked up a china jug and was filling it with warm water from a big kettle on the stove. She placed the jug on the long kitchen table, went to a drawer and took out squares of clean white cotton. She pulled out a chair and indicated that Bodie should sit down. He did and the girl busied herself bathing the gash of his skull.

"This town has suffered long enough because of Frank Lowery and his bully boys. You should know how they treat people. How long had you been in town when they took you over to the gaol? And what had you done?"

"Turns out I asked the wrong sort of questions."

"And for that they crack your skull

and toss you in a cell!" The girl gave a bitter laugh. "Welcome to Elkhorn. A nice, safe town — providing you live by the Major's rules!"

Bodie winced as her fingers pressed sharply on the raw gash. "Hey! I got clouted once today because of that feller! And that was one time too many!"

"Sorry," the girl apologised. "I didn't mean to take it out on you."

"Appears to me the Major ain't one of your favorite people," Bodie said. "You want to tell me why?"

The girl finished bathing his wound. She washed her hands, then moved to pour out a couple of cups of coffee. Handing one to Bodie she sat down at the table, absently stirring sugar into her drink.

"Why do you want to know?" she asked.

"Because the Major is part of the reason I came to Elkhorn."

The girl's eyes widened, settling firmly on Bodie's face. "I'd like to hear that reason."

"Back down the mountains is a town called Pine Ridge?"

The girl nodded. "I know it."

"More than a week ago a feller got himself killed there. He was a local rancher. He got into an argument with some men. Later they caught up with him, dragged him in an alley and knocked him around — and then one of them blew him apart with a shotgun. They shot another feller in the leg when they quit town."

"Go on."

"The four men involved were Jody Butler, the Major's son, feller named Lee Haddon, one of the Major's hands, and a couple of other fellers who work for him. The town council in Pine Ridge put out a bounty for Jody Butler and the others, and that's where I come in."

"I see," the girl said slowly.

"Bounty hunter ain't always the kind folk fancy sitting in their kitchen," Bodie said. "I can leave if you want."

"Lord, no," the girl said quickly. "You just stay where you are. Tell me, how long have you been after them? I only ask because I've seen Lee Haddon around town a couple of times over the last few days, and he didn't appear to be looking over his shoulder."

"That's because he doesn't figure he's got anything to worry about," Bodie said. "I caught up with them a couple of days after they'd left Pine Ridge. But they got the drop on me." Bodie touched his still-bruised face. "They worked me over pretty good, tied me on my horse and sent me back to Pine Ridge. I think the idea was to persuade anyone else with the same idea to forget it."

"It doesn't seem to have persuaded you."

Bodie smiled tightly. "One thing I never did learn was how to quit. And when I'm advised in such a persuasive way I just can't help myself from coming back and trying again."

"Does Frank Lowery know that's the

reason you're in Elkhorn?"

Bodie shook his head. "We didn't get as detailed as that in our conversation. Seems I didn't act humble enough for him, so I got clouted over the head and left in a cell. I overheard that Lowery had gone to bring the Major to town. I figure they were interested because I'd been asking the way out to the Butler spread."

"The way things are in Elkhorn right now, that's enough to get you hung from the nearest tree," the girl said.

"My turn to ask why?"

"I'll tell you — but first I want to know who I'm talking to. My name's Fran Skellhorn."

"Bodie."

Fran frowned slightly. "First or last?"

"Just Bodie," he said, indicating there was no more to be added.

"All right, Bodie. If you've ridden through this area you'll know this is all cow country. Some of the best. It's been that way for a long time. The only bad thing about this country is Howard

Butler — the Major. He's a powerful man. Wealthy. Has a lot of influence. He's also ambitious and greedy. And he's not particularly concerned if he hurts anyone who happens to get in his way. I'm sure you've heard about his hold over this town. The fact that he owns a large part of it. Many of the people around town are under his influence one way or another."

"You an exception?"

Fran smiled. "Actually, yes. This place is all mine. It came to me when my mother died about three years ago. The Major has never bothered me. Probably because the business is too small to be worth his attention. Anyhow that's the situation in town. The main reason behind the troubles we're having right now is the proposed spurline the railroad wants to run through the mountains into Elkhorn."

"Surely that's good?"

"Yes. A spurline would bring wider opportunities to Elkhorn. Increased business investment and the like. More people, more money. And it would mean that the local ranches — and mainly the Major's — would be able to ship their cattle direct instead of having to trail them all the way down to Pine Ridge. It would save time and money — again a good thing."

"But — ?"

"But in the process of putting in the spurline the railroad would have to cut through Kittyhawk Creek. That's a large section of range northeast of town. There are about eight independent ranches who work that range. Solid, well established outfits who have been there for many years."

"There's no other way for the railroad to come through?"

Fran shook her head. "No. The mountains to the north have been surveyed throughout. The only possible route for the spurline has to cut right across the Kittyhawk Creek range. It would destroy the rangeland and wipe out every outfit there."

"I take it that the Major is all for the spurline?"

"He heads the Elkhorn Development Company, along with the bank. They stand to gain most from the spurline."

"But the ranchers along the Kittyhawk won't budge?"

"No. Why should they? Give up what's taken a lifetime to build? Sell out knowing that no matter how much money they make, they'll never find such good land again? And money isn't everything, Bodie. To some people it's the land that matters. The homes they've built. The families they've raised. It's easy for the Major to talk glibly of the public good — would he give up his land if the spurline could only come in across Butler range?"

"That's a question I'll ask him when I see him," Bodie said. "Is the Major putting pressure on the Kittyhawk people?"

"Oh yes," Fran said. "It started about three days ago. Midnight raids on the ranches. Hooded riders burning barns.

Spelling it out that the next time it might be bodies that are burning. One of the Kittyhawk ranchers was beaten when he tried to run the riders off. Cattle have been scattered. Fences torn down. It's so pointless. The Kittyhawk people have formed themselves into an alliance and they'll fight Butler for as long as it takes."

"You sound pretty involved yourself," Bodie pointed out.

Fran caught herself, face flushing. "Was I on my soapbox? Well, there's no reason you shouldn't know, Bodie. I am involved. My uncle, Amos Skellhorn, is the man leading the fight against the Major. He's been fighting Butler for years over all kinds of things. It's no secret that the Major has had his eyes on the Kittyhawk for a long time. But there isn't a thing he's ever been able to do. Every spread on the Kittyhawk is legally owned, right down to the last blade of grass, by each man who runs an outfit. If the truth were known, it's probably the Major who doesn't have legal title to all the range he's taken."

Somewhere in the building a clock chimed softly. Fran glanced up, startled, rising from her seat.

"Heavens, I've got work to do!" She snatched up an apron from the table and tied it about her waist. "I'll show you the room upstairs and then get ready to open up. As soon as I can I'll bring you something to eat."

"Don't worry about me," Bodie said. "When I close up we can decide what's best for you." Fran stopped speaking for a moment, her eyes raking Bodie's face. "You do trust me? Don't you, Bodie?" she asked.

"Yeah," he said. He lifted the cup he was holding. "When somebody can make coffee as good as this you can't do anything but trust them!"

8

FROM the window of the small bedroom above the restaurant Bodie was able to observe the nightlife of Elkhorn in comparative comfort. He'd only been up there for a half hour when Frank Lowery rode in. Lowery was accompanied by an older man — probably in his early fifties — who carried himself as if he had a steel backbone. There was something in the manner of the man, the way he looked about him, the brusque motion of his hand when Lowery asked a question, that told Bodie he was looking at Howard Butler — the Major himself.

By the time Lowery and the Major arrived back in town, the initial fuss over the shooting at the gaol had died down. Contrary to what Bodie had expected, there was little organised search for him. Bodie had watched the body of the deputy called Rick being carried out and taken away up the street. Shorty, his arm in a temporary bandage and sling, eventually came out of the gaol with the doctor. Together they vanished into the darkness. That seemed to leave the third deputy — Vinnie — on his own. He appeared in the doorway of the gaol with a couple of tough-looking characters who took the rifles he handed them, gathered their horses from the hitch rail and mounted up. Vinnie gestured in various directions and the two riders moved off up the street. After that things got fairly quiet again, and nothing of much interest occurred until Elkhorn's law returned.

Lowery and the Major dismounted and went inside the gaol. The heavy door to the office closed and stayed closed. Bodie would have given his right arm to have been a fly on the office wall at that time. Whichever way the story was told, Frank Lowery was going to come out of it looking a damn fool. And that wasn't going to add to his fondness for Bodie. The manhunter grinned into the dark room. The hell with the whole bunch, he thought. I hope they all have a bad night!

The Major stayed in the gaol for over an hour. He finally emerged, slamming the door shut, and striding across the boardwalk. In the saddle he rammed his heels into his horses's sides, causing the animal to pull against the reins. For a moment it seemed as if the animal might overcome its rider in the struggle. But the Major, by sheer will power and brute strength, hauled the animal's head round, and held the trembling horse motionless. He sat there for a moment, as if daring the horse to question his will again, then jabbed in his heels and rode off up the street, into the pool of darkness that lay beyond the gaol.

That seemed to be that, Bodie decided. He moved away from the window and sat down on the edge of the soft bed. He unbuckled his gunbelt, hanging it over the back of the wooden chair standing beside the bed. He made sure that the Colt and the knife were both easy to get at. He leaned the Winchester against the wall on the other side of the bed.

Stretched out on the bed he let the silence envelope him. Below he could pick out the muted sounds from the restaurant. He found himself thinking about Fran Skellhorn. When he'd seen her earlier, while he'd been eating, he hadn't given her more than a passing acknowledgement. Her ready grin had concealed her true personality. Bodie had seen her as little more than a gawky, not-too-beautiful young woman. His second meeting with her had dispelled those impressions. Fran Skellhorn had an agile brain inside that head of hers, and there was more to the girl than might be initially apparent. On a more basic level he found himself wondering why he found himself attracted to her — because he'd realised that he was. She had an open manner liable to frighten off many men — those who preferred a woman to be totally subservient, without the kind of abrasive quality that Fran Skellhorn possessed. Maybe it was that part of her that Bodie liked.

He had drifted off into half-sleep, his body taking the opportunity to catch up on some of the rest he was denying it. Then his deep rooted instincts warned him something was different, and Bodie came awake instantly, snatching the Colt from its holster, hammer going back, loud in the silence.

And that was it!

The silence! Complete, almost a physical sensation, reaching out to envelope him.

Bodie sat up, listening for a moment. Then he relaxed, easing the hammer down on the gun. Damn fool! He shook his head. The reason for the silence was below him. In the deserted restaurant. Deserted because Fran had closed up for the night, locking the doors behind her last customer. Bodie swung his feet to the floor, working some of the stiffness out of his body as he stood up. He moved to the window and checked the street. Empty except for a couple of stragglers wending their way home. He eyed the gaol. Even the office light had been extinguished. The building was in darkness.

There was a soft tap on the door. Bodie crossed the room and opened it. Fran Skellhorn stood there, framed by the landing light, a tray in her hands.

"I've brought you some coffee," she said. "And a plate of sandwiches. I hope you like cold beef and homemade pickle."

"Sounds fine," Bodie said, taking the tray from her.

Fran closed the door and went to peer out of the window. "I saw the Major come and go. Seems they aren't too concerned about finding you."

Bodie, pouring himself some coffee, glanced up. "I don't reckon that's the end of it."

Turning from the window, Fran folded her arms, watching him eat. "It might sound funny, Bodie, but it's a little unsettling to have a man up here. This used to be my room. I ... I've only ever had one other man in here."

"You make it sound like you regret it."

She smiled. "No. It's just that it was a long time ago."

"No friends nowadays?"

"One or two people I know."

"Nobody special?"

Fran shook her head, her eyes revealing the inner yearning. "Not in that way," she said. "There was — but things change, and people — and then I had to take over the restaurant when my mother died. It doesn't leave much time for socialising."

"You expecting to keep the place going forever?"

A bitter smile edged Fran's mouth. "You only get so many chances in life, Bodie. Like I said — mine didn't work out. Who knows, maybe it was my fault."

"He run off with somebody else?" Bodie asked directly.

A brittle gleam shone in Fran's eyes. "Yes, dammit! Does it show so obviously?"

He glanced up at her. "What?"

"My inability to attract a man!"

"Hell, no, Fran," Bodie said. "You got no call to say that about yourself."

"Don't try and fool me, Bodie. I'm no raving beauty and I don't have enough grasp of the spoken word to sparkle with wit and conversation."

"You reckon that's a good enough excuse to bury yourself behind a kitchen stove for the rest of your life?"

Fran stared at him, as though a truth had just dawned on her. "Is that what I'm doing? Maybe you're right, Bodie." Then she sighed, shoulders slumping. "I said I lost my chance. So I have to live with it." She hesitated, reluctant to take her point to its natural conclusion. "But living with it isn't always easy.

I'm a healthy woman and it's a lonely life sometimes, Bodie . . . and I think you could be in the same situation too. So you'll know what I'm talking about."

Bodie didn't speak. There was no need. He could appreciate her position, and he was sympathetic with her situation. It had to be harder for a woman. Much harder.

Fran crossed to the door and left the room quietly.

Bodie sat alone in the semi-darkness with his tray of food and his dark thoughts.

Later he had a quick strip-wash with the water Fran had left for him in the tall jug on the dresser. Dumping his clothes on the chair beside the bed he slid under the cool sheets. He lay for a while, listening to the soft sounds of Fran moving about in one of the adjoining rooms. Then even that noise ceased. Bodie settled down, sleep drifting over him slowly.

He heard the door of his room

open. Bodie reached out and grabbed the Colt, swinging it in the direction of the door, his finger easing back the hammer. Then just as quickly he relaxed and lowered the gun.

Soft lamplight from the landing outlined Fran's tall figure. She had loosened her thick hair, allowing it to hang down her back. Gently she closed the door as she slipped into the room, padding across the floor. The bed creaked softly as she lowered herself down beside Bodie, drawing the covers up to her neck. He felt the smooth firmness of her naked hip and thigh against his body.

"All I want is a few hours, Bodie," she said out of the darkness. "No strings. No recriminations. Not even a thank you. Just the time between now and morning . . . "

Her warmth roused him as she turned her body to him, hands reaching out to touch him, fingers trembling. Bodie held her gently and Fran gave a low cry that might have been relief — or even fear — as he ran his hands across and down her naked back, over the swell of her buttocks, caressing the long, tense thighs. She twisted over on to her back, pulling his face down to hers, soft, moist lips parting beneath his. Bodie cupped his hands over the soft breasts, fingers teasing the rising nipples. Fran squirmed against him, lifting her strong hips. A sharp, expectant gasp came from her as she became aware of his risen hardness thrusting against her flat stomach.

"Oh, Bodie," she whispered in a voice that betrayed her aching loneliness. "It's been such a long, long time!" And then she eased apart her thighs for him. Bodie guided himself to the heated moistness, carefully entering her until Fran relaxed enough for him to penetrate fully. Then she let out a long, shuddering groan, arching her strong thighs over his hips. She began to thrust her hips and buttocks up off the bed, straining violently as if she needed to get Bodie even deeper inside her. In the darkness of the room, out of the closeness of their coupling, rose a hoarse, ragged expelling of breath. The sound came from Fran's lips, deepening and strengthening as she approached a rising climax. As the spasm took her the husky breathing ceased. Fran threw back her head, the taut flesh of her face glistening with sweat, mouth open to release a long, much welcome cry of pleasured relief. The sound lingered, floating in the shadows above the gently creaking bed, and soon there was no sound at all.

9

"THERE'S my uncle's place."

Bodie followed Fran's finger. He could make out the shape of a long, low house sheltering in the leafy shade of tall trees. As Fran set the team in motion, taking the buckboard on along the trail, approaching the ranch, he was able to see that Amos Skellhorn's place was more than just a small outfit. The ranch buildings were well built, cleanly painted, the whole place organised and self-sufficient. It was obvious why Skellhorn had refused to move out and why he had refused financial compensation. Money couldn't buy what had gone into this outfit. The man's life had built the place. There was his sweat and probably his blood, too, in the ranch, and asking a man to put a price on it was like asking him to put a price on his newborn child.

As they rolled into the yard fronting the house the door swung open and a tall figure stepped out, the sunlight glinting on the barrel of the rifle held in large, work-hardened hands.

"Uncle Amos," Fran called. "You put that thing down now. This is a friendly visit."

Amos Skellhorn lowered the rifle, striding across to the buckboard, a wide smile on his brown, craggy face. He wore a thick, dark beard that covered the lower half of his face but which failed to hide the still-healing bruises marking his cheeks. As Skellhorn reached the buckboard he stared past Fran, his wary eyes raking Bodie's face closely.

"Who's he?" Skellhorn asked.

Fran stepped down off the buckboard. She touched Skellhorn lightly on the shoulders and kissed him on the cheek. "He is a friend," she said. "His name is Bodie, and he's come looking for Jody Butler and some of his partners in crime."

"Crime? What crime?" Skellhorn asked, puzzled.

"Murder," Bodie said. "Butler and three of his friends killed a man back in Pine Ridge a while back. I've come to take 'em back there."

Skellhorn digested the information for a moment. "You taking 'em dead or alive?"

"The way feelings are between them and me I can't see it being anything else but dead. When they see me they'll know they ain't about to get a second chance — not after what they did to me the first time we met — and I ain't about to go sending invitations out before I start shooting."

"Bodie, I'm beginning to like you," Amos Skellhorn said. "Come on inside, the both of you, and we'll talk over some coffee."

The inside of the house was up to the standard of the exterior. Amos Skellhorn led the way through to the large kitchen and indicated chairs they could use. He brought cups and a large pot of coffee. When he'd poured three cups and seated himself at the head of the table Skellhorn gave Bodie another long, searching look.

"You hear about our problems?" he asked.

Bodie nodded. "Only thing I can't figure is why you're just sitting back and letting them come to you. Why not take the fight to Butler? Give him a taste of what he's handing out to you."

"Fran, I like this man," Skellhorn said. "Hell, Bodie, I wish you were with us! I've been trying to get my people to do just what you suggest. But they reckon we're doing enough by digging in our heels and refusing to let Butler intimidate us."

"A man like Butler understands one thing. Direct action. Ain't no damn good just shaking your fist at him. You've got to let him feel it. Make him taste his own blood. Hurt him."

"He means what he says, Uncle

Amos," Fran interrupted. "Bodie hadn't been in town long before Frank Lowery threw him in gaol for asking questions about the Major."

Skellhorn threw a sharp glance in Bodie's direction. "And you got out?"

"It wasn't hard."

"Lowery's deputies tried to stop him. Two of them are hurt and Rick Jenner is dead."

"Well that's one who isn't going to be missed," Skellhorn said. "Bodie, you play a hard game. Right now, though, I wouldn't want to change places with you. The Major takes it pretty hard when a man working for him gets hurt. He'll be in a hanging mood."

"That's nothing fresh," Fran murmured.

"Oh?" Bodie asked.

"By now you'll have figured out the way Butler runs Elkhorn. Pretty much his way. And there are times when it gets a little rough. There've been a number of hangings over the past few years. All done by Butler's so-called

Regulators. Hell, the man must think we're stupid. Everybody in the territory knows the Regulators are Butler's men hiding under hoods. They're nothing but a bunch of killers!"

"Up to now they've only hung rustlers and horse thieves," Fran said. "No trials. They just picked them up, rode into town and hanged them. It was terrible to see."

"I've got a feeling that's what they have in store for some of us on Kittyhawk Creek!" Skellhorn said. "Butler's bound to make another move. And when he sees that what he's doing now hasn't moved us, he'll try something else. And somebody is going to end up dead sooner or later!"

"So let it be some of them and not you," Bodie told him. "Next time you . . . "

His final words were lost in the brittle crash of breaking glass as one of the windows at the front of the house shattered.

Bodie grabbed his rifle and followed Amos Skellhorn through the living-room. Glass littered the floor near the broken window and a large rock lay on the rug in the centre of the room.

Stepping to the side of the broken window Bodie peered out and saw a straggling line of horsemen ranged across the yard. He counted nine of them, every man armed, and all of them wearing crude white hoods over their heads and shoulders.

"Amos Skellhorn, step out here!" one of the hooded men yelled.

Bodie glanced at Skellhorn, who was standing at the other window, his face dark with anger.

"Comes a day when you've got to decide who's running your life, Skellhorn," he said.

Amos Skellhorn hesitated, but only for an instant. And then he lifted his shotgun, driving the muzzles through the glass. Before the glittering particles had touched the ground Skellhorn's shotgun exploded with heavy sound, a gout of flame and smoke erupting from one barrel.

A hooded rider rolled sideways out of his saddle, the front of his shirt blossoming with spreading scarlet. The rider crashed to the ground and lay twitching in a pool of his own blood, his chest pulped to the bone by the devastating power of the shotgun blast.

There was momentary confusion amongst the riders. It was obvious that they were not used to the idea of someone actually fighting back, and it had left them temporarily at a disadvantage.

"Hit 'em!" Bodie snapped. "Now — while they're thinking about it!"

He thrust his rifle through the window and started shooting, raking the line of riders with a deadly volley. He emptied two saddles, his bullets tearing bloody gouts of pulped flesh from jerking bodies. A third rider skewed half out of his saddle, barely managing to stay on his horse, clamping a hand over the blood spurting wound in his shoulder.

And then the riders fell back. Horses were jerked round, protesting against the heavy use of reins and spurs. A few desultory shots were fired in the direction of the house as the riders drew to a safe distance.

Amos Skellhorn grunted in satisfaction. He opened his shotgun and replaced the spent shell. "Damn," he said forcibly. "You didn't give me much chance for a second shot there, Bodie."

The manhunter grinned. "Times like these, Skellhorn, a man's either very quick or very dead."

"They're leaving," Fran called.

Bodie glanced out of the window and witnessed the riders trailing away from the ranch, dust rising in pale clouds in their wake. The yard outside the house lay silent, though not empty. There were three riderless horses — and three dead men.

"Stay in the house, Fran," Skellhorn

said. He opened the door and strode across the yard with Bodie at his rear.

Reaching the first corpse Skellhorn reached down and ripped away the man's blood-spattered hood. He studied the face for a moment, nodding to himself.

"He one of Butler's men?" Bodie asked.

"Sure. Name of Brittles." Skellhorn stood upright. "Didn't know one end of a cow from the other, but he damn well knew all about guns."

They removed the hoods from the other two men. Bodie saw a face he recognised and pointed it out to Skellhorn.

"Name of Travis," Skellhorn said. "You met him before?"

"He's one of the four I'm here for. He was in on the killing back at Pine Ridge. And I owed him for a few hard knocks."

Skellhorn glanced at the gory hole Bodie's bullet had punched in the chest of the man called Travis. "I reckon you paid him in full, Bodie!"

With Skellhorn's help Bodie loaded the bodies on to the three horses, roping them down.

"Be obliged for the loan of a horse," Bodie said.

"Take your pick," Skellhorn said. "I'll have Fran make up a sack of supplies. I take it you aim to go after Jody?"

"It's why I'm here," Bodie said.

"Ain't going to be easy. Hell, Bodie, you'll be a target for every gun on Butler's payroll! Let me come with you, man. I know this country. Every rock and every damn hole. And so do Butler's gunhands."

"You've got a job," Bodie pointed out. "Looking after your property. You've hit Butler hard today, so he ain't going to be so casual about it next time. But don't ease off, Skellhorn. You see a Butler man riding in you put a bullet through the son of a bitch. Call in your hands. Set up a defence line. Gather your stock and push it all in a place you can protect easily. Make Butler pay for every inch of your land he even looks at, and maybe — just maybe — he'll leave you alone!"

"Sure you wouldn't like to come and work for me?"

Bodie shook his head. "I couldn't stand the pace, Skellhorn," he said. "I like a steady life."

A wide grin split Skellhorn's face. "The hell you do!"

Later, as Bodie finished saddling the big dun mare he'd chosen, Fran came into the stable. She was carrying a loaded sack of supplies and a big canteen of water. Handing them to Bodie she stood back and silently watched him complete his preparations.

"I didn't get a chance to say thanks," Bodie said suddenly.

"For what?"

"Sneaking me out of town the way you did." Bodie turned from the horse. He saw Fran's troubled expression.

"Something bothering you? Hell, did I forget to pay for my bed and breakfast?"

Fran's eyes sparkled and her mouth curled up at the corners. "Maybe I should charge you," she said. "After all, you did rather take advantage of the little extras I offered!"

"Seems to me, Miss Skellhorn, that those extras could get to be catching."

Fran moved across to him, pressing her supple body close. Without any encouragement she put her arms round his neck and touched her lips to his.

"See," she said a short time later, "you're doing it again."

"What?"

"Why — taking advantage of me — again."

"Honey, I'd love to be around when you do it of your own free will," Bodie said, and reluctantly disentangled himself from Fran's embrace. "Now you get the hell out of here and let a man tend to his business."

"Bodie, don't you realise how crazy

you're acting?" Fran gripped his arm. "You've just seen the sort of thing that happens round here. Butler's men aren't playing games. You can't go up there after Jody all on your own. Not against Butler's whole crew!"

"He ain't about to come down to me," Bodie pointed out. "Look, Fran, we agreed last night. No strings. No reasons why. Far as my job goes that's the only way it can be. I can't afford the luxury of allowing myself excuses why I shouldn't do this or that. I start counting up the risks I'm going to be too damn scared to even climb out of bed to put my pants on."

Fran took a slow step away from him, knowing that she had no right to erect distractions. She was breaking her own rule about not getting involved, a rule that Bodie himself worked by. She was aware of the kind of man he was. Independent. Self-sufficient and totally in control of his own destiny. He was no man to be tied down, hemmed in by a fleeting thing like emotion. She had accepted that the night before, when she had gone to his room — but now, in the light of day, fully aware of her own feelings, she admitted that her need for him had already gone beyond a single night of passion. In the same realisation she also faced the fact that for Bodie the episode might well be over and already forgotten.

"Just take care, Bodie," she said, and hurried out of the stable, keeping her face turned away from him, so that he wouldn't see the shine of tears in her eyes.

When Bodie led the horse outside some minutes later Fran was nowhere to be seen. But Amos Skellhorn came out of the house and crossed over to speak with the manhunter.

"I been doing some thinking, Bodie," the rancher said. He held a rolled map in his hand, which he now opened. "This here is Kittyhawk Creek. My place is there. You ride west. Here you'll be on Butler land." He indicated various landmarks. "Now after you cross the high meadow above Cascade Lake there's a hell of a climb to the western rim of Butler's range. Cut slightly north and you'll have the Cascade Hills in front of you. Way up on top is what they call round here The Major Canyon. Butler has a line-shack up near the canyon. Hard to get to. Pretty isolated. Hell, in winter a man can be stuck there for a couple of months. I figure that's where Butler's got Jody. Hiding him out until he can figure some way of getting the boy off the hook for that killing. And given time that's just what the Major will do. One way or another he'll buy Jody's freedom."

Bodie took the map and studied it, committing to memory all the landmarks and distances. "Looks to be a couple of days' ride up there," he said.

"Closer to three," Skellhorn said. "Like I told you, that's rough country up there. Nothing for miles but hills and forests. Why a man could spend a lifetime up there and never see another human being."

"Times are when that wouldn't be such a bad thing," Bodie said.

He mounted up and rode his horse over the yard to where the three corpses hung over their saddles. He picked up the loose reins and glanced towards the house. The door opened and Fran stepped out, smiling at him.

"Take care," she said again.

Bodie nodded at her. "Get her back to town," he said over his shoulder to Skellhorn.

"I intend to." Skellhorn held out a big hand, gripping Bodie's firmly. "I have the feeling I'll be seeing you again."

Bodie touched the dun's sides and set off across the dusty yard. He pointed the horse to the west, settling in the saddle. He didn't look back. He never had seen the point in looking back. What was past was dead, didn't matter any more, and though the future might not have a deal more to offer at least it was alive, it had purpose, and sometimes it had promise.

10

THE breathless heat of high summer hung over Bodie like a stifling blanket. The rising folds of the hills above him lay in a permanently shimmering haze. Even though he was riding through thickly wooded areas most of the time there was little escape from the heat. Reining in beside a swift flowing, narrow stream that tumbled and splashed in and out of the rocks and grass, Bodie eased out of the saddle and dropped to his knees. He took off his hat and thrust his head into the water, gasping and spluttering against its icy contact with his flesh. He straightened up, shaking water from his hair as a dog might shake its coat. Scooping up water in his palm he drank it down, feeling it tingle against his teeth. He climbed to his feet, sleeving water from his face. Far below him he could see the mirror gleam of water that was the Cascade Lake. He had ridden by there the day before. Now he was faced with the lofty peaks of the Cascade Hills. Amos Skellhorn had been right. It had been a hell of a climb to get this far, and the worst was yet to come.

He had ridden away from Skellhorn's ranch and off Kittyhawk range, finding his way across the endless spread of land that came under Howard Butler's rule. Bodie had ridden until he'd spotted one of the well-defined trails that criss-crossed Butler range, and here he had turned loose the three horses and their grisly loads. Someone from the Butler ranch would spot them eventually and take them in. Once he'd disposed of the bodies he had drifted on across Butler land, keeping to ground with plenty of cover. The last thing he needed at that time was to get himself spotted. By the evening of that first day he had reached the comparative safety of the foothills, and with the grey light of the dawn he was out of his blanket, in the saddle, and already starting the long climb before the sun had risen.

Once or twice during his ride he had seen riders in the distance. But he had been expecting to see Butler men, so his mind was working in advance, again keeping him close to cover, maintaining a line of travel which kept him off any skyline ridges as far as was possible. And his preparedness paid off, always allowing him the time to gain cover before any distant rider could spot him.

Despite the fact that he was high up now, deep in rough, trail-less country, Bodie didn't allow himself to relax his vigilance. Foolhardiness was not one of his failings. Howard Butler would be the kind of man who would demand constant and thorough patrolling of his range, from border to border. His men could appear anywhere and at any time, and Bodie didn't relish the idea of rising smack into a couple of ready guns simply because he let his guard down. The cemeteries were full of men who let go too soon, figuring they had all the angles worked out. It never did to let yourself believe you were on top. That was the time when some sneaky son of a bitch went and hammered you right into the ground. If a man allowed that to happen to him, then he had no damn right calling himself a professional, and if he wasn't a professional then he shouldn't have been in the business in the first place. Amateurs were fine when it came to playing the piano — but there was no place for them when it came to wearing a gun.

Bodie jammed his hat back on and climbed back into the saddle. He waited until the dun had finished drinking from the stream, and then gathered his reins and pushed on towards the steeply rising, rugged slopes before him.

He leaned forward and drew his Winchester out of the scabbard, checking that the rifle was primed and ready for use. For the last hour or so he'd been restless, plagued by a feeling of not being alone. He hadn't seen a thing, or even heard a sound to indicate that his instincts were telling him the truth. Even so Bodie decided that caution was better than a bullet in the back of the head.

Ahead of him and slightly to his right a bird rose out of thick brush. Bodie kept on his forward course, giving no indication that the bird had given him warning. But at least now he knew where part of his problem lay. The bird had taken flight through being frightened.

Bodie took the dun along the edge of a shallow basin, its bottom choked with grass and brush. He was almost clear of the rim when his eyes, still centred on the thick brush ahead, picked up the merest suggestion of a human shape in amongst the intertwined vegetation. His suspicion was confirmed when the grey bulk moved and sunlight flickered briefly on metal.

Bodie slipped his feet out of the

stirrups and he rolled off the dun's back, dropping over the edge of the basin. As he hit the grassy slope he heard the hard slam of a rifle shot. A bullet whacked the edge of the rim, showering him with dirt. Bodie relaxed and let himself roll into the thick brush growing part way up the side of the basin. He twisted over on to his stomach, jamming the butt of the rifle to his shoulder.

A man's voice, raised in an angered yell, cut the silence, the sound of the echoes prolonging the outburst. Brush crackled and popped as a heavy body forced its way through. A second voice called out. Bodie smiled, baring his teeth. The stupid fools! All that damn shouting and yelling! Giving away their positions every time they opened their mouths!

A distorted figure appeared on the rim of the basin. A face leaned over, eyes peering down into the shadowed mass of brush.

Bodie put a single bullet through the

man's head. It entered just above the left eye, drove on through the skull and angled upwards to blast its way free in a gout of blood and brains. The man threw up his arms, almost as if he was appealing to God in his last moments, and then he fell back out of sight. There was a long silence after the sound of the shot, and then Bodie heard a soft drumming sound coming from beyond the rim of the basin. He recognised it after a moment. It was the noise made by the dying man's boot heels kicking on the dry earth. After a time the sound ceased.

One down, Bodie counted, but how many more were there? One he was sure of. But there could have been others, wiser men who had the sense to keep their mouths closed and their eyes open at a time like this. He decided it might be better for his state of health if he got out of the basin. If there were more and they got him surrounded things could become awkward.

Bodie crawled across to the far side of the basin and edged his way up the slope. There was a heavy spread of brush that reached to the top of the slope, so he was able to make it to the rim under cover. He slid over the rim and worked his way deep into the thick brush growing along the edge of the basin. When he was far enough in amongst the tangle of roots and leafy branches he turned his body about. And then he waited.

Long minutes drifted by. Heat drove down through the tangled brush, striking at Bodie through his shirt. Sweat oozed greasily from his pores. Bodie suffered in ungracious silence, flicking beads of moisture from his face.

He spotted the first man coming down off a low rise, moving slowly as he approached the far side of the basin. The man was still yards away when another figure appeared, rising from where he'd been lying in thick grass. The pair converged on the basin from opposite directions, each glancing at the other in anticipation of some sudden action.

Bodie slid the muzzle of the Winchester through the brush, sighting on one of the approaching figures. He had been definite in his choice of target, because he had recognised a familiar face. One of the men was Brenner — he'd been with Jody Butler and Lee Haddon when they'd got the drop on Bodie and used him as a punching-bag. Bodie had trained his rifle on the other man. He didn't want Brenner dead — not just yet.

The Winchester nudged his shoulder as Bodie tripped the trigger. The bullet struck its target dead-centre, lifting him off his feet and throwing him back a couple of yards. The man hit the ground on the back of his neck, his hurt body twisting violently in reaction to the terrible pain. He came to rest against the thick trunk of a tree, his blood marking a glistening trail across the lush grass.

The moment Brenner heard the

shot he dropped to a crouch, his own rifle starting to bear down on Bodie's position. But the manhunter's Winchester was already lined up on Brenner's body. He eased the muzzle to one side and put a bullet into the ground a bare inch from Brenner's boot.

"That could have been in your stomach, Brenner!" Bodie called. "The next one will be! And I don't waste time bragging — if I say it can be done it's the truth! Now it's up to you, feller! If you want to die just go ahead and use that rifle you're holding!"

Brenner's face remained stonily impassive. He was staring in Bodie's direction, though it was obvious he couldn't see the manhunter. It was what was going on behind that face that interested Bodie. It could have saved him a lot of trouble if he'd been able to read a man's mind. To know what was being thought and planned long before it took place.

"I ain't waiting all day, Brenner!

Make your mind up, feller, 'cause my trigger finger's gettin' tired, and if it slips you're going to have an extra belly button — one that runs from front to back!"

"You bastard!" Brenner yelled, for no other reason than it made him feel a whole lot better.

"All right, Brenner, now you've shown me you know a big word. So see if you can understand me — get rid of the rifle! Now!"

"Hell, you son of a bitch, how'd I know you got the drop on me?" Brenner wailed.

"Easy way to find out," Bodie said. "Go ahead and make your play, feller. If you hear me yell you've won. If you don't it ain't goin' to make all that much difference to you what happens next!"

"Goddamn it!" Brenner shouted. He stared at his rifle and then flung it from him wildly. "I done it — you son of bitch — I done it!"

"Now the handgun," Bodie said.

Brenner lifted his revolver from the holster and tossed it into the basin. He held out his empty hands. "You mean son! Ain't right to make a man throw away his gun! By God, that just ain't nice!"

Bodie climbed to his feet and stepped carefully around the rim of the basin. He walked around the sprawled body of the man he'd shot while he'd been down in the basin, kicking the dead man's gun out of sight. Brenner watched him in sulky silence, his dark eyes full of reproach.

"Bodie, I wish we'd finished you first time we met," Brenner said.

"Found out who I am too?"

Brenner smiled. "Don't take the Major long to find things out. It was as easy as just sending a telegraph message to Pine Ridge. The Major has a lot of friends in a lot of places."

"An undertaker one of 'em?" Bodie asked.

"Why?"

"The way I see it the Major's going

to be needing the services of one pretty soon!"

"Hah!" Brenner sneered. "Bodie, you must be a fool! The Major's got more men than he knows what to do with! Mister, you stand a snowball's chance in hell of gettin' close to Jo . . . !"

Bodie's big right fist curved round and clubbed Brenner across the jaw. Blood sprayed from Brenner's mouth as he went down. He was still trying to get up when Bodie booted him in the side, spinning him over on to his back and cracking a couple of his ribs. Brenner lay staring up at the manhunter. His mouth hung open, blood trickling from split gums.

"Jesus, Bodie, that was damn sneaky," he mumbled, biting back against the rising pain from his broken ribs.

"Brenner, don't even thank me," Bodie said. "I ain't even started yet!"

He leaned over and took hold of Brenner's thick hair, dragging the moaning man to his feet. Brenner clutched his side, eyeing Bodie distrustfully.

"All right, so I got it comin'," he said. "Why don't you just shoot me and be done!"

"And miss all the fun we're having?" Bodie said, and drove his fist into Brenner's face again. Something cracked with a loud noise, blood gushing down Brenner's face. He dropped to the ground, hugging his body, and shook his head violently.

"Shit, you miserable bastard, that's it! I ain't gettin' up again, so if you got a mind to shoot me you better just do it!"

The smile that appeared on Bodie's face did little to make Brenner feel any easier. The expression seemed to imply that Bodie's thoughts were running along the same lines.

"Is Jody up at the line-shack, Brenner?"

Brenner rubbed a hand across his bloody mouth. "Even you can't get to him, Bodie. The Major's got him boxed in tight." Something made Brenner smile. "Hell, it's all bein' done to keep that little shit out of gaol, but the way things are he's locked up tighter than any damn cell's likely to hold him!"

"Well don't worry on my account," Bodie said. "Gaol's get busted into as well as out of."

"I ain't worryin' for anyone but ol' Brenner. Look, Bodie, I don't give a damn what happens to that little asshole. Even the Major don't rate him too high, but he'll protect him 'til hell freezes over. Me — I'd sooner bury him with the rest of the shit."

"Brenner, for somebody who doesn't like Jody Butler, you been workin' awful hard tryin' to keep me off his back."

"You take a man's pay, Bodie, you do his work. Mind, it wasn't all for Jody Butler. I'd only go so far risking my neck for that little pissant. I ain't no fool, Bodie. I knew damn well you'd be gunnin' for me as well as the others. My skin's valuable to me. So I aimed to protect it."

"You should have tried harder,

Brenner," Bodie said. "That's one of the drawbacks in this line of work. A man pays dear for his mistakes."

Brenner raised his head slowly, the implication of Bodie's words dawning with increasing clarity on his numbed mind. He stared into Bodie's grim face, and knew that he was facing death. For a moment he appeared to resign himself to the fact — but with startling ferocity he burst into movement, hurling his body to the side, across the grass, his bloodstained fingers reaching out for the rifle dropped by one of his dead partners. It was a futile gesture, but it was the only thing Brenner could do apart from sitting back and letting himself die like some crippled old man.

The Winchester in Bodie's hands blurred as he swung it round, the muzzle fixing on Brenner's moving form. The rifle fired, white powder-smoke ripping from the shot. The side of Brenner's skull caved in under the impact, flesh and bone mingling with the thick gout of blood that errupted from the dark hole. Brenner stiffened, his body slamming hard against the ground. As the bullet emerged from the opposite side of his head there was an ugly gush of blood and brains, shattered bone and pulped flesh that sprayed across the green grass around Brenner's body. Brenner kicked for a while and the fingers of one hand clutched at the grass, tearing it from the very earth. But it was a futile attempt to hold on to life, and it ended the moment Brenner's heart stopped beating.

Bodie turned and walked to where his horse stood cropping grass, oblivious of the violence and death around it. He jammed his rifle back in the sheath and climbed into the saddle. Taking up the reins he put the horse back on the route he'd been covering before. He jerked the brim of his hat down to shade his eyes. It was still a hot day and he still had a damn long way to go.

11

THE lineshack stood in the shadow of the canyon's wide mouth. Beside it was a lean-to and corral holding half a dozen horses. Close to the canyon wall a clear spring bubbled up out of the bedrock, feeding a natural, deep rock pan. Smoke rose from the tin-pipe chimney sticking up through the roof of the shack.

Bodie, stretched out on a flat rock overlooking the lineshack, familiarised himself with the general layout of the place. Since he'd been watching the lineshack there had been a fair deal of movement in and around the place. Armed men came and went, carrying out the normal, everyday chores that were part and parcel of spending time in an isolated spot such as this. The horses in the corral were fed. Wood was chopped for the shack's stove, water brought from the spring. On the surface it all looked calm and peaceful, as natural a scene as anyone could ask to see.

But it was all as phoney as hell. Every man who came out of the shack, on whatever errand, was as tight as the drawstring on a miser's purse. They moved as if they suspected trouble from every blade of grass, their eyes flitting back and forth, probing shadows, suspecting any flicker of motion. They were obviously being paid very well to see that no harm came to Jody Butler, and from the way they were acting Bodie figured they'd start shooting if Howard Butler himself rode up unannounced.

Bodie drew away from the edge of the rock and climbed down to where he'd left his horse. He felt a rising throb of pain coming from his ribs. He tried to ignore the feeling. He knew he hadn't done any good coming off his horse the way he had back down the mountain. He reached solid ground and went to his grazing horse. The big dun lifted its head and stared at him as if to ask why they were moving on now it had found a good place to eat. Bodie snatched up the reins and swung into the saddle. The dun held back a little when he touched its sides. Bodie tightened the reins and rammed in his heels. The dun, deciding that a half-empty stomach would be easier to live with than aching ribs, moved off.

Bodie took a direct route that brought him out on the far side of the corral, using it as a barrier between himself and the lineshack. He freed the coil of rope hanging on the saddle and flipped the noose over the top of one of the corral's main posts. Easing the dun away from the corral Bodie let out all the slack, snubbing the last few feet around the saddlehorn. The dun stopped dead when she felt the rope go taut. Bodie touched her sides and the dun took the strain. Bodie kept her going, slowly. He felt the rope twang. The dun hesitated and then stepped on. Bodie heard the grumble of sound coming from the thick post. On an impulse he slid his Winchester from the scabbard and laid it over his thighs. The rope creaked softly. Bodie dug in his heels and the dun lunged forward. The post came up out of the dusty ground with a rush, thudding to the ground and dragging down side-poles on either side. Loosening the rope from his saddlehorn Bodie took the dun into the corral, got behind the milling horses and triggered off a single shot from the Winchester. The horses panicked and bolted from the corral in a trailing cloud of thick dust. Bodie followed them out, so that by the time the lineshack's door was flung open, he was clear of the corral and swinging round it to meet the armed men who burst through the door.

His first shot ripped through the thigh of one gunman, kicking him off balance and dumping him face down in the dust. The man lay wriggling about in the dirt, trying to stem the thick stream of blood gushing from the ragged hole. Lying over the dun's neck Bodie thundered across the open ground, scattering the line of gunmen, firing as he swept by them. He felt the close passage of their returned fire.

As he went by the shack Bodie caught a quick glimpse of a figure standing in the open doorway. It was a fleeting image, a white face staring up at him, but there was no mistaking the identity of the man.

Jody Butler.

Reaching the far side of the corral Bodie dropped from the saddle, letting the dun run on. He flopped belly down in the dust, jamming the Winchester to his shoulder, and triggered a fast shot at the first of the gunmen to turn and face him. The bullet caught the man in the throat, blasting out through the back of his neck in a gush of pulped red flesh. The gunman went over backwards, his own gun going off as his finger jerked back on the trigger.

Dust was beginning to thin out as Bodie rose to his feet and ran across to the meagre shelter of the lean-to. He heard a rapid volley of shots. Bullets whacked the earth around him. One burned a hot slash of pain across the upper muscle of his right arm. Then he reached the cover of the lean-to and threw himself behind it, twisting his body over so that he rolled on to his feet.

He could hear the slap of booted feet coming in his direction. Bodie grinned to himself. It was like chickens just waiting to be slaughtered. The gunmen were so anxious to earn their big fat bonuses they were forgetting the simple rules of survival. Bodie jacked a fresh round into the Winchester's breech — well he sure as hell wasn't going to remind them what they were doing wrong.

He heard the nearest of them approach the lean-to, close in.

Bodie held back, finger tight against the trigger.

Waiting...

Listening... gauging the man's position.

And then he stepped into the open... gun up and ready...

A look of surprise crossed the gunman's face... his eyes registered his dismay... he knew he'd made a mistake... one that was going to cost him dearly...

The Winchester blasted a single shot — the bullet tearing away the left side of the man's face. Exposed bone gleamed stark white for a fleeting moment before a bubbling wash of blood spilled forth. The stunned gunman stumbled awkwardly, throwing up his hands to try and stem the torrent of blood gushing from the raw hole in his face. As he started to go down Bodie shot him again. A bullet over the heart that tumbled the man into the dust, his blood spattering the ground with big, dark stains.

Bodie turned about as a lean shape came around the far end of the lean-to, a levelled shotgun grasped in white-knuckled hands. Continuing his movement Bodie lunged forward and down, dropping below the level of the twin muzzles. He heard the solid blast of sound as one barrel discharged, felt the hot wind of the shot howl over his head. Then he hit the ground, his body jarring from the impact. He tilted the Winchester up, firing off a shot that put a bullet through the gunman's groin. The man screamed, a long, shrill howl of agony as the bullet ripped up into his body. It entered on the left side, angling off to the right impacting against the hip bone. Splintered bone burst out through the exit wound, punching out globules of bloody flesh and sinew. The screaming man fell back against the lean-to, dislodging a rack of saddles and harness as he fell. Despite his severe wound he managed to retain his grip on the shotgun, and as Bodie came to his feet the gunman jerked his finger back against the second trigger. The shotgun boomed with a heavy roar, spitting a gout of flame and smoke at Bodie. The manhunter felt the burning sting of shot tear across his side, then the flood of hot blood that coursed down his body. He swung the Winchester in a short curve, pulling the trigger as the muzzle pointed at the gunman's head. The bullet blew the face apart, bursting the brain out through the back of the shattered skull.

Cutting round the end of the lean-to Bodie made a dash for the rear of the lineshack. He'd almost reached the shelter of the building when a gun opened up from over by the corral. Bullets peppered the earth around his feet, whacking up dusty spouts of dirt. Lowering his shoulders Bodie took a wild dive for the protection of the shack. He hit hard, grunting as pain surged up around his sore ribs. Rolling, he got his feet under him and lunged upright, pressing his back tight against the plank wall of the shack. Sweat poured down his grimed face. Chest heaved as he sucked air into burning lungs.

Silence fell . . . and stayed . . . then was broken as a man began to moan softly. Bodie remembered the gunman he'd shot in the leg. That had been a bad misjudgement, but at the time he hadn't the opportunity to do anything further.

The manhunter eased his way along the rear of the shack, aiming for the far end. He rounded the side of the shack and stepped cautiously to the front corner. He peered round, and saw the wounded man, still sprawled in the dirt. There was a lot of blood still coming from the jagged wound in the man's thigh. The man was lying on his back, both hands clutched over his thigh, but he wasn't having much effect on the flow of bright blood.

Bodie was more interested in the man who had been shooting at him from the corral. As Bodie spotted him the man rose to his feet and started to move towards the far end of the shack. He was so intent on what he was doing that he wasn't aware of Bodie's presence until it was far too late.

The gunman's head snapped round as Bodie stepped into view and pulled the trigger of the Winchester. The bullet took the man through the middle, doing a lot of damage internally before it burst out of the man's back, blowing apart his spine. Blood and bits of pulped flesh and bone spewed out of the big, ragged hole, and the gunman did an ungainly, jerky dance, as his upset nervous system reacted to the shock of the bullet's passage. Then his limbs lost all their strength, cut dead by the shattering of his spine, and he flopped limply to the ground, his upper body twitching in ugly spasms.

Bodie walked across to where he lay and the gunman stared up at him through pain-dulled eyes. Blood frothed from his wet lips.

"Don't leave me like this," he begged, and his wish was granted by a single bullet that tore his heart to shreds.

A sharp rattle of sound made Bodie turn. The gunman with the leg wound had hauled himself to a sitting position and had somehow retrieved his fallen gun. He was struggling to draw back the hammer of the heavy revolver, but his hands were thick with blood and his grip was loose. He was swearing softly, forcibly as he tried to yank back the hammer. His head was bent over the gun and he seemed oblivious to the fact that he was advertising his intention with the subtlety of a man banging on a bass drum. Bodie shot him through the head and then retraced his steps to the lineshack.

The shack's door was closed tight against him. Bodie put down his rifle and took out his Colt, checking that it was primed before he put his shoulder to the door and drove it clean off its hinges. He went in low, diving to the left as he cleared the step, hitting the floor on his shoulder and rolling.

A gun blasted, loud in the shack's confining space. The bullet ripped a chunk out of the doorframe, a second wild shot followed it.

Bodie came up on one knee, his Colt rising almost with a motion of its own, and settled on the figure of Jody Butler, who was crouched in the far corner of the shack, wide eyed and oozing cold sweat from every pore. For a split second Bodie held his aim, then moved the Colt a fraction before touching the trigger and putting a bullet through the soft, fleshy part of Jody's right arm. Blood gushed from the entry and exit wounds, spurting thick and red. It soaked Jody's sleeve and spattered his shirt and pants. Jody let out a terrified scream and fell back against the wall. He took one look at the pulsing, bloody holes in his arm and lost control of himself. A large, dark wet stain spread across the front of his pants.

On his feet Bodie crossed the shack, kicking Jody's dropped gun out of reach. He reached down and caught hold of Jody's hair, dragging the screaming, crying man out of the shack. He hauled Jody outside and dumped him in the dirt. Jody curled up in a whimpering, cowering ball. He began to beg for help, tears streaming down his red face, and Bodie stood the noise for as long as possible. When it got on his nerves he rapped Jody behind the ear with the barrel of his Colt, and after that it got very quiet.

It would have been so easy to have killed Jody Butler. The thought ran through Bodie's mind as he stood over the motionless figure. Too damn easy! Putting a bullet into Jody's skull would have been the painless way out, but Bodie figured there was little or no justice in that. It would suit his purpose to keep Jody alive — long enough to deliver him to Pine Ridge, and the tender care of Jonas Wayland. And keeping Jody alive would act as bait in getting Lee Haddon out from wherever he was hiding. Haddon had been mainly responsible for the savage beating Bodie had suffered, and Bodie liked to settle personal scores. He had a long memory when it came to evening up outstanding debts.

By the time Jody Butler came round he was tied in the saddle of a waiting horse. His arm still hurt badly but the bleeding had stopped. There was a bandage round the arm as well. Jody ran his dry tongue over equally dry lips. Jesus, I need a drink, he decided, and remembered the bottle of expensive whisky he'd been emptying while he'd been in the lineshack.

"Hey, Bodie, where are you? Come on, you bastard!"

"You just keep on that way, boy, and it's going to be my pleasure to knock you out of that saddle!"

Jody's head snapped round and he looked into the grim face of the manhunter. Bodie, mounted on his own horse, had moved up alongside Jody, and he was sitting closer than Jody would have chosen — if he'd had a choice in the matter.

"I want that bottle of whisky out of the shack," Jody demanded. He lifted his tethered hands. "And get these ropes off me, you son of a bitch!"

Bodie shook his head in disgust. "Can't understand the younger generation," he said. "Ain't a shadow of respect in any of you." And then his left hand swept up and round. The backhand slap caught Jody full across the mouth, rocking his head back, and if he hadn't been tied there Jody would have rolled out of his saddle. As it was he slumped sideways, head dropping forward on to his chest, blood dribbling from a split lip. "Now you listen to me, boy. You ain't in no position to smart-mouth me. You better get it through your head that if I take it in my mind to kill you, then I can do it, and there ain't any way I'm liable to answer for it. Don't matter how I deliver you to Pine Ridge — dead or alive. I still pick up my bounty money. So you think on, boy. Makes no damn difference to me. Brenner and Travis are dead. They both took the hard way to go. I've got you, so there's only Haddon left, and I don't figure it'll be too long before I settle with him."

Jody raised his head slowly. He stared at the sprawled, dead bodies of the gunmen his father had surrounded him with. Fat lot of help they'd been, he thought. He swivelled his eyes to the side and studied Bodie carefully.

"You won't get me off this mountain alive, Bodie," he sneered.

"Then I'll get you off dead," was all the reply he received.

"Why waste your time? My father ain't about to let you take me all the way to Pine Ridge for a hanging! If you knew the Major, you'd know he don't let anyone ride over him!"

"Boy, I ain't interested in meeting your old man. I've enough on my hands with the pissant he fathered! Last thing I need is some jumped-up cowman trying to play fancy games."

Bodie reached and took hold of the reins to Jody's mount. He touched the dun in the sides and led off, skirting the corral and making for the timbered hills beyond.

"Damn it, Bodie, you take me to Pine Ridge they'll hang me for sure!" Jody's voice rose to a wild screech. "Goddamn it, you listen to me! I ain't no two-bit outlaw you can drag from hell to breakfast!"

"Boy, I know who you are, and it sure is a pain in the ass! Now either shut your miserable mouth or I'll do it for you!"

Jody fell silent and remained that way for some time. They rode up into the shade of the timber, the horses' hooves making no sound as they trod the floor of the forest where thick layers of leaf-mould created a muffling carpet. It was a long time later when Jody broached the matter he'd been deliberating during his silence.

"Bodie — hey, I want to talk."

"Yeah?"

"How much are they offering?" Jody asked.

"Who?"

Jody scowled at Bodie's feigned ignorance. "The Pine Ridge Council — that's who. How much is the damn bounty they've put up?"

Bodie glanced over his shoulder. "I don't think I ought to tell you, boy," he said.

"Hell, why not?" Jody asked indignantly.

"Wouldn't want to embarrass you, boy!"

Jody stiffened. "You sayin' they didn't lay out a big enough bounty?"

"No!" Bodie stated flatly. "Ain't that so much. Way I look at it they went and offered too damn much for you, boy! I figured that at the time, and since I set eyes on you I know I was right. Boy, you are a sorry sight, and I'm damned if I can see 15,000 dollars worth in your carcass."

"Well, the hell with you, Bodie, 'cause somebody did!" Jody crowed.

"Don't put too much store in that,

boy," Bodie said. "Only reason for all that money is because they want you to pay a return visit to Pine Ridge. Only for a short stay mind." A bleak smile edged Bodie's hard mouth. "I don't reckon they'll keep you hanging around for long!"

12

"THEY'RE all dead, Major. Every last one of 'em."

For a moment Lee Haddon was sure that Howard Butler was going to strike him. The expression in Butler's eyes was terrible to see. He hunched his shoulders and closed his hands over the saddlehorn, holding back the rage that was threatening to explode into uncontrollable violence. Gradually he calmed himself down, aware that he was being watched by every man riding with him. Howard Butler was no fool. He knew what was expected of him and he had no intention of allowing his feelings to reveal themselves in front of his crew. He raised his eyes and picked out Lee Haddon.

"Is Jody there?" he asked, and saw Haddon's negative shake of the head. "So we must assume that this bounty hunter has him."

"I picked up the trail of a couple of horses that were ridden out from the lineshack," Haddon said. "Heading east."

"All right," Butler said to his waiting riders. "You heard that. Ride out and start looking. I want Jody found and I want that damn bounty hunter."

Lee Haddon watched the riders move off. He shifted uncomfortably in his saddle, waiting for Howard Butler to look his way.

"Major, this is my fault, and I feel bad about it."

"How can it be your fault, Lee? It wasn't you who allowed Bodie to break out of a cell. If Lowery had done his job properly we wouldn't be in this mess now."

"And if I'd dealt with Bodie that time we had him," Haddon said, "none of this would have happened."

Butler shook his head. "You acted correctly under the circumstances, Lee. I don't fault you there. At that time another killing wouldn't have helped. But circumstances alter and we have to change our approach."

Haddon swore softly. "Jesus, if I'd know who it was Lowery had got locked up in a cell . . . !"

"Yes, it was unfortunate that we didn't find out until Bodie had made his escape. However that is behind us now. What we have to do is look ahead, and do some thinking. I'm certain now that it must have been Bodie at the Skellhorn place. Somehow he's become involved with Skellhorn and the rest of those Kittyhawk upstarts."

"It's possible he's found out about your trouble with them," Haddon said. "He was in Fran Skellhorn's place just before Lowery's deputies picked him up. She could have told him about the troubles."

"I always suspected there was more to that girl than she ever showed," Butler murmured. "You know, Lee, I'm damn sure she helped him that night he broke gaol. Lowery's boys scouted the country for miles around town. But they couldn't find a damn track anywhere. And Bodie didn't pick up his horse from the livery. It's still there. Yet he was out at Skellhorn's place next morning when Lowery took that bunch in to throw another scare into Amos."

"All that got thrown was a lot of lead," Haddon said.

Howard Butler suddenly began to smile. "Lee, I think we can work something out that might get Jody out of trouble."

"What's that, Major?" Haddon asked.

Butler spurred his horse into motion. He waited until Haddon had fallen in alongside him. A faint smile curved up the corners of Butler's mouth.

"Look at the facts, Lee. Bodie has got Jody. He has a reputation for always delivering his prisoners — dead or alive. Money won't mean a thing to him — except the money he picks up as bounty."

"So?" Haddon asked, not getting the

meaning behind Butler's words.

"So we need something to bargain with, Lee. We have to face the fact that we're up against a professional in Bodie. It's no use treating him like some two-bit saddletramp."

"All right, Major, tell me what we bargain with!"

Butler only smiled. "You'll see," he said.

They cut off across the open rangeland, riding steadily for the rest of the day, and it was close to dusk by the time they entered Elkhorn. Butler reined in outside the gaol, dismounting and tethering his horse. Lee Haddon did the same and followed his employer inside. Frank Lowery was seated behind his desk, busily engaged in cleaning a revolver he'd got stripped down and spread out before him.

"Major," he said, glancing up as Butler came into the office. "Something wrong?"

"Bodie got to the lineshack," Butler said heavily. "And he didn't let those damn hired guns stop him. Right now he's somewhere on the way back to Pine Ridge with Jody."

Lowery's face paled visibly. He knew he was still in Butler's bad books for allowing Bodie to break out of the gaol. "Anything I can do, Major?"

"Two things," Butler snapped. "Get every man you can out looking for Bodie and my son. But I don't want any action taken that might put Jody in danger. I'll hold you personally responsible for enforcing that order, Frank. Understand?"

"Sure, Major."

"When you've done that I want you to ride out to Amos Skellhorn's place. Tell him I want to see him here in town, and make him realise it's vital he comes. If he refuses, bring him — but I don't want him brought in beaten to a pulp. I want him sitting his saddle and able to ride."

Lowery snatched up his hat and hurried from the office without a word.

"Dammit, Major, I wish you'd tell

me what you got in mind," Haddon said.

"Let's go eat first," Butler said. He led the way out of the gaol and started to cross the street.

"Hotel's the other way," Haddon pointed out.

"Didn't I tell you, Lee?" Tonight we're going to eat at Fran Skellhorn's place."

"Hell, Major, you never eat there! You always tell me you . . . "

Butler glanced round as Haddon's voice trailed away. "At last," he said. "For a time there, Lee, I was beginning to think you'd lost your way."

Now it was Haddon's turn to grin. "Major," he said, "you're one crafty son of a bitch . . . Fran Skellhorn! I should have guessed as much."

They stepped inside the restaurant. It being early evening there were already a number of customers occupying tables. There were a few raised heads and more than a few raised eyebrows when Butler was recognised, but there wasn't a word said as Butler and Lee Haddon made their way to a table in one corner.

They had been there for a few minutes when Fran emerged from the kitchen, carrying a loaded tray. As she moved over to serve the diners waiting for the food, her gaze moved around the room and came to rest on Howard Butler. For no more than a fraction of a second she faltered, her face puzzled, but with superb control she recovered her composure and went on to serve the food. This done she crossed the restaurant and stood at Butler's table.

"What can I get you, Mister Butler?" she asked.

"Your best meal," Butler said, smiling. "For two."

"You sure that's all?" Fran asked. "How about one of the Kittyhawk ranchers stuck on a spit and being roasted over my stove? I see that more to your taste."

"Thank you, Fran, I'll keep it in mind," Butler said. "But for the moment we'll make do with plain food."

After Fran had returned to the kitchen Lee Haddon glanced at Butler. "How have you got this planned?"

"Oh, nothing elaborate, Lee. For the time being we act like any other customers. Just take our time with the meal and wait for the place to empty. There's usually a lull around eight. When we're alone you go and lock the door, pull down the blind, and then we have her."

"Amos Skellhorn ain't going to be too happy," Haddon pointed out.

"That's true. But then I'm not in the happiness business, Lee, and I don't give a damn one way or the other about Amos Skellhorn's feelings."

It was almost ten minutes past eight when the door closed behind the last customer. Lee Haddon shoved aside his cup of cold coffee and stood up. He crossed the restaurant in quick strides and locked the door, jerking down the blind. Fran, who had been standing behind the counter, looked up as she heard the key rattle in the lock.

"Haddon, what're you up to?" she demanded.

"He's just doing what I told him to do," Butler said. He stood up, smoothing down his coat. "I must congratulate you on a fine meal, Fran. I really never knew you were such a good cook."

Fran gave him an icy stare. "And you had to have the door locked and the blind down just to tell me that?"

Butler stroked his chin, feeling his fingers rasp against hard stubble. "Not exactly," he said. "You see I didn't want anyone to walk in right now."

"Oh? Why? You going to take off your clothes and do a dance across the tables?"

"Me?" Butler shook his head. "I'm sure Lee wouldn't object if you indulged in such an entertainment. But my purpose is a little more serious, Fran. What it boils down to is that you are now my hostage, and you will remain so until your friend, Bodie, returns Jody to me alive and well."

"My God, Butler, you really are getting desperate," Fran said.

"You could be right, Fran. So I suggest you treat the situation with all seriousness. Because, Fran, I am not playing."

"No — you're just plain crazy!" Fran yelled. "You can't go round taking people prisoner just like that! I really do think you have gone mad!"

Butler's face hardened, muscles twitching in his cheek. He took a sharp intake of breath, and then without warning his right hand came up and round and he slapped Fran across the side of the face. There was enough force behind the slap to thrust Fran back against the counter. She almost lost her balance, but managed to retain it by clinging to the edge of the counter.

"Perhaps you will choose your next words with care," Butler said.

"You can count on that," Fran said severely.

"Bring her along," Butler snapped to Haddon. "Let's get out of this place."

They left by the rear entrance, moving along the shadowed backlots until they were level with the gaol, waiting until the street was deserted and then walked directly across to and into the gaol. Haddon shoved Fran inside and Butler closed the door as he followed them into the office.

"Now sit down and keep your mouth shut," Butler said. "Unless you want to spend some time in one of the cells back there."

"Some choice," Fran murmured and perched herself on one of the hard seats.

Howard Butler smiled suddenly, rubbing his hands together like an excited small boy. "The way things are working out, Lee, we could resolve a couple of pressing problems here tonight."

"Yeah?" Haddon remarked. He was helping himself to a cup of coffee from the blackened pot on top of the small stove in the corner of the office.

"It came to me that having Fran here where we want her might just be enough to persuade Amos to sign over his property to me. He thinks a lot of Fran and he wouldn't want to be instrumental in causing her any grief."

"Hell, that could work out fine," Haddon said.

Butler nodded. "I can't figure why I never thought of it before."

"Maybe you were too busy evicting little old ladies and hanging the odd saddletramp," Fran said bitterly.

"We live in a hard country, my dear," Butler said conversationally. "Rough justice often serves the needs of the community."

"Rough justice?" Fran laughed. "Is that a legal term for out and out brutality and cold blooded murder?"

"You're letting imagination colour your thinking, Fran. Be honest . . . how far would western expansion have got if men hadn't been bold enough to act harshly when the situation required it? I think you have to accept the rough and ready code of the kind of civilisation we live in, Fran. It'll be a long time before this country is tamed, and until then, if a man wants to make his way, then he's going to have to live in a dog-eat-dog world."

Fran didn't bother to reply. She had realised that there was no way of convincing Howard Butler of his total disregard for human life. He was one of the breed of men all too frequent in the frontier communities. Hard, ruthless, unfeeling men, all bitten by the same bug, with a need to build and expand, to gain power and wealth by any and all means. Men who twisted and manipulated the law, used their wealth to purchase the means by which they could wrest from the rightful owner whatever they decided they wanted. Violence and corruption were daily fare for these men. They saw something, desired it, and took it, by whichever method suited that particular deed.

And they had no scruples when it came to using underhand means. Fran leaned back in her seat and fixed her gaze on the gaol's closed door. She had a feeling she might be here for some time yet.

Over an hour passed before anything happened. The gaol door opened and Amos Skellhorn stepped into the office. Frank Lowery was close behind him, a rifle in his hands.

"Fran! You all right, girl?" Amos Skellhorn asked as he spotted Fran. "Damn you, Butler, if you harm her I'll . . ."

"Whether or not Fran comes to harm is in your hands, Amos," Butler said. "Do what I ask and Fran can walk out of here untouched. Play stubborn, and I promise you, Amos, that you'll regret it."

"You son of a bitch!" Skellhorn roared. "By God, I was right the day I called you a madman. And when I called this place Hangtown."

"I had a feeling it was you who

coined the phrase," Butler said. "But that is water under the bridge, as they say. Right at this moment in time, Amos, I have only one thing to say to you — find Bodie and bring him and my son back here, and while you're doing that you'd better think about changing your mind about selling out to me. Remember that Fran's life depends on you making the correct decisions in both cases, and be certain sure, Amos, that I am in deadly earnest over this. I've no time to waste and the deaths of a few insignificant people don't bother me in the slightest!"

Amos Skellhorn looked deep into Butler's eyes. He saw the intense, bright stare, recognised the mark of a fanatic, and accepted the fact that Howard Butler meant every chilling word he'd spoken.

13

BODIE saw the rider coming down off the ridge above him and drew rein to watch. There was something familiar about the man but he was too far away for Bodie to recognise. One thing he was certain of — the rider wasn't hostile. If he was he had a damned original way of sneaking up on a man. Even so Bodie made sure his rifle was ready for instant use, because despite outward appearances it didn't pay to treat any situation as anything but potentially threatening.

The appearance of the rider aroused Jody Butler's attention. He'd fallen into a sullen mood of silence right from the moment they had ridden away from the lineshack, and the past couple of days had gone by with hardly a word from him. Now he raised his head and watched the lone rider pick his way down the long slope.

"Boy, I wouldn't get too excited," Bodie said. Whoever he is he ain't about to do me any harm."

In a way Bodie was wrong. The rider turned out to be Amos Skellhorn. He rode in with both hands empty and in plain sight.

"Bodie, you are a hard man to track," he said.

"That's the idea," Bodie told him. "And you're a long way from home, Skellhorn. There must be a good reason why."

Amos Skellhorn nodded. "Yeah. But I ain't so sure about it being good." He threw a grim look at Jody Butler.

There was something in Skellhorn's manner that alerted Bodie, and he wasn't too surprised by Skellhorn's next words.

"Bodie, you've got to take Jody back to Elkhorn!"

Jody Butler gave a low chuckle.

"Shut your mouth, boy," Bodie

warned. "Skellhorn, there's need for a reason why."

"Is Fran's life reason enough?"

"Butler got her?"

Skellhorn nodded. "He's holding her. And the only way to get her back is to hand Jody over to the Major."

"I said you wouldn't get me off this mountain," Jody crowed.

Bodie swung round on him. "Boy, I won't tell you a second time. And who said things have changed?"

"Don't bluff me, Bodie," Jody sneered. "You can't . . ."

Bodie hit full in the mouth, his bunched fist smashing Jody's lips back against his teeth in a splatter of red. Jody gasped and rolled back out of his saddle. His hands were tied so he couldn't break his fall. He hit the ground hard and lay still.

"Never known anybody with so damn much to say!"

"Bodie!" Skellhorn begged.

"Ease off," Bodie said. "What's Butler's deal?"

"Jody back alive — then he lets Fran go."

"That ain't all . . . is it?"

"No."

"I didn't figure Butler to let you off so easy."

"He wants my signature on the sale of my spread."

"Now there's a son of a bitch who likes to twist the knife." Bodie glanced curiously at Skellhorn. "No?"

Skellhorn shrugged. "I can always find more land," he said.

Bodie sighed. "Seems I could have saved myself a lot of trouble. Chasin' all over these damn mountains after that little pissant — and now I have to give him back!"

Skellhorn's tension drained away. "Bodie, I was startin' to believe I'd have to fight you for him!"

Bodie's unshaven face creased into a wry grin. "And you would have done too!"

Skellhorn helped Bodie haul the unconscious Jody back on his horse.

As they began the long ride back to Elkhorn, Skellhorn said: "I don't trust him, Bodie."

"Man would have to be a damn fool if he did."

"Butler's a vindictive man. He can't stand his authority being challenged in any way. Hell, Bodie, you've done nothing but walk over him since you arrived. He won't let you ride out once he's got you in Elkhorn." Skellhorn put a hand on Bodie's arm. "Let me take Jody in alone. Ain't no call you gettin' hurt on my account."

Bodie shook his head. "Doesn't work that way," he said. "Day I let another man shoulder my risk is the day they can bury me. I had to go back anyhow. Seems I forgot about picking up Lee Haddon. Memory must be slipping."

Amos Skellhorn didn't push the matter. He couldn't quite make up his mind about Bodie. Of one thing he was sure — there was a reason why Bodie was going back to Elkhorn, and it sure as hell had nothing to do with memory — or the lack of it.

They rode through the night, resting for a couple of hours just before dawn. After a quick cup of hot, strong coffee they moved on. The spreading light from the rising sun followed them across the green mountain slopes as they trailed in towards Elkhorn.

Mid morning placed them in sight of the town, and Bodie brought them to a halt.

"Why we stoppin'?" Jody Butler asked. His lips were still badly swollen from Bodie's punch and his speech was muffled.

"I got arrangements to make," the manhunter said, climbing out of his saddle. He made sure Jody's hands were still securely tied. With extra lengths of rope Bodie lashed Jody's feet in the stirrups.

"What's goin' on, Bodie?" There was a slight, but rising, panic in Jody's tone.

"Boy, don't be so all fired anxious. Bide your time."

Satisfied that Jody was secure Bodie mounted up again. He turned to Amos Skellhorn.

"Be obliged if I could borrow that scattergun," he said. Skellhorn handed the shotgun over. Bodie checked it, finding both barrels loaded. "Thanks."

Jody's face had turned a sickly white. He glanced at the shotgun, then up at Bodie. "What you aimin' to do with that thing?"

"There you go again, boy. That curiosity of yours is going to get you into trouble — any minute now."

Bodie swung the shotgun round and jammed the twin muzzles up under Jody's chin, the cold steel sinking into the soft flesh, forcing Jody's head up. There was a hard sound as Bodie eased both hammers back to full cock.

"Got the idea now, boy?"

Sweat beaded on Jody's face, trickling down his flesh in glistening globules.

"Nothing to say now? Ain't you the contrary one. Mind, it's the advisable thing to do, boy. Say the wrong thing and I'm liable to let you have both barrels. And that wouldn't be healthy — apart from giving you a permanent cure for headaches!"

Bodie urged his horse forward, keeping Jody's alongside, while Amos Skellhorn fell in at the rear. They angled down a slight bank and came on to the regular trail that brought them in through the outskirts of Elkhorn.

There were a lot of interested spectators who stood and watched the silent trio riding in. Bodie scanned the staring faces, wondering who amongst them might work for Howard Butler. His interest was created not out of fear, but out of a knowledge that an itchy trigger belonging to a man anxious to earn Butler's bounty money could upset the whole damn apple cart. But it was a risk he had to take. He was here, in Elkhorn, deep in Butler's territory, and when a man was as committed to an action as Bodie was, then there was no turning back.

As Bodie neared the jail he saw an

armed man lounging on the boardwalk. The man spotted the approaching riders, stepped forward to get a closer look, then turned and vanished inside the gaol. He reappeared after a minute, followed by a half dozen other men. Bodie recognised Frank Lowery and Lee Haddon among them.

"Looks like a reception party," Bodie said, glancing at Jody. "That's real nice of your daddy, boy!"

Jody kept his mouth shut tight. He was terrified of making any movement which might trigger off the shotgun jammed painfully into the soft flesh of his chin.

A dark suited figure moved to the edge of the boardwalk, hands resting casually on his hips.

"The Major," Amos Skelhorn said.

"So you're Bodie!" Butler said. There was a grudging respect in his voice, a cursory trace of admiration for Bodie's professionalism, if not for the end result of his ability. "You've caused me a great deal of inconvenience."

"Still intend to keep it up," Bodie said. "I hear they still call you Major — do I say hello or salute you?"

A shadow of a smile etched itself across Butler's face. "Humour as well?"

"Hell, yes. It writes and reads too, and it learned a long time ago not to be fooled by horseshit passing itself off as something special."

Butler's face paled slightly. "All right, Bodie, let's get down to the matter in hand. We all know what we're here for. You want the girl — I want my son."

"For a smart feller, Butler, you don't seem to be getting much out of this deal. This little pissant ain't worth the flea off a dog's back." Bodie gave the shotgun a slight thrust, ripping a ragged moan from Jody's swollen lips. "You certain you want him back?"

"For a smart man yourself, Bodie, you don't seem to appreciate the difficult position you are in." Butler glanced at the men behind him. "One nod from me and you're dead."

"So is he," Bodie pointed out. "You

know damn well I'll pull both these triggers even if you cut me in half."

There was a long silence as each side weighed up the position.

"So now we've threatened each other and called each other nasty names how about dealing, Butler?" Bodie flexed the arm holding the shotgun. "The longer you drag this on the stiffer my arm's going to get . . . "

"For God's sake . . . " Jody blurted out, ignoring for a moment the threat of the shotgun. "He'll kill me . . . I know him and he'll do it!"

"Skellhorn, you ready to sign?" Butler asked.

Amos Skellhorn climbed down off his horse and stepped to the boardwalk. "You damn well know I am."

Howard Butler took a folded document from his pocket. "I figured you'd see sense, Amos. Let's go inside. You can put your name on this deed and I'll give you your money and Fran."

They stepped inside the gaol, leaving

Bodie alone for the moment. He watched Frank Lowery edge forward.

"You got away from me once, Bodie," Lowery said. "You won't do it a second time."

Bodie glanced down at him. "I wouldn't have thought you'd got time to stand and talk, Lowery."

A frown creased Lowery's face. "What do you mean?"

"I figure you should be inside there with Butler. Must be at least five minutes since you licked his ass!"

Lowery's face darkened. He lunged forward, his hand snatching at the gun on his hip. He would have drawn if Lee Haddon hadn't reached out and caught hold of his wrist, forcing the gun back into the holster.

"You crazy son of a bitch," Haddon rasped. "Hell, are you so dumb you can't see when a man's proddin' you! Judas Priest, Frank, you want to end up gettin' hung with one of your own ropes?"

"I ain't about to let no bastard

talk to me the way he did!" Lowery yelled.

"Here and now, you let him say just what he damn well pleases!" Haddon said. "Or do you want to be the one who tells the Major that Jody's just had what brains he's got blown the length of the street?"

There was a murderous gleam in Bodie's eyes as he watched Frank Lowery, a silent warning to the lawman that he was ready if any trouble started. Lowery allowed himself to be pushed back across the boardwalk until his shoulders were rubbing against the gaol wall.

"Son of a bitch!" the Elkhorn lawman grumbled sourly.

The jail door opened and Amos Skellhorn came out. Close behind him was Fran. She looked tired, her shoulders hunched and her head down. Skellhorn said something to her and she glanced up. When her eyes caught Bodie's she gave a quick smile and lifted a hand to brush at her loose hair.

Howard Butler pushed his way to the front of the men bunched on the boardwalk. He seemed pleased with himself, and for some reason that angered Bodie.

"There's the girl," Butler said. "My part of the bargain, Bodie."

"Skellhorn, get Fran out of here!" Bodie said sharply.

"Now hold on!" Lee Haddon swung round to face the manhunter, his gun halfway out of its holster.

"Ease off, Haddon," Bodie warned. "Take the advice you just gave Lowery."

Behind Bodie Amos Skellhorn was pulling Fran on to his horse. Skellhorn took up his reins and began to edge his horse away from the gaol.

"Bodie?" he said urgently. "Let's get out of here!"

"Take Fran and move out!" Bodie snapped without moving his eyes off the grouped men on the boardwalk. "Do it!"

Howard Butler held himself from making any comment. He had seen the expression on Bodie's face and there was no escaping from the solid fact of the shotgun pressed so tightly beneath Jody's chin.

"Bodie, we made a bargain," he said after a while.

Bodie could see Skellhorn's horse moving further and further along the empty street. Fran kept looking back, her face pale, and while he'd still been able to read them her eyes had held a pleading look — as if she had been silently begging him to follow.

"A bargain, Bodie," Butler repeated.

"The hell we did, Butler! You just gave an order and just naturally expected we'd all come running! You must figure I'm pretty dumb if you think I'm about to put away this shotgun and expect to ride out free and easy."

"Do you have any other choice?" Butler asked.

"Damn right I do, mister! You might have this whole town jumping through hoops every time you whistle — but this is one dog that never did take to doing tricks. I'm going to give you a choice, Butler. You can choose whether or not your boy dies right here on this street or leaves town with me and takes his chances back in Pine Ridge!"

"You make a fool of me, Bodie, and I'll track you to the front door of hell!" Butler screamed. He jabbed a finger at the manhunter. "You hear me, you bastard!"

Bodie picked up his reins. "Sure I hear you, Butler, and seein' you all upset really makes my day. Now back off or I'll put both loads through the boy's head!"

"Kill him and you're a dead man, Bodie," Lee Haddon said.

"Either way I'm in for a hard time, so I might as well play my best card. Now back off!"

Bodie touched his heels to his horse and it stepped away from the boardwalk. He pulled the reins of Jody's mount, drawing it in close to his side, so that he had Jody between himself and the men on the boardwalk. As Bodie walked his horse along the street the bunch, led by Howard Butler and Haddon, began to follow along the boardwalk. The empty street suddenly looked a mile long and Bodie felt a cold sheen of sweat form on his face. If his scheme worked he decided he'd be happy to come out of it with his skin intact — if it didn't he figured Howard Butler would want more than just his skin.

Halfway along the street, and Bodie was almost ready to believe he might pull it off. There was still a way to go and it would be far from over even when he'd cleared town — but he figured there was a chance.

That was until a gun went off somewhere behind him!

The bullet ripped a bloody furrow across the top of Bodie's left shoulder. His horse lurched forward, startled by the sound of the shot, and Bodie's finger was jerked against the shotgun's triggers.

The weapon exploded with a solid blast of sound, both barrels firing together. The full charge of the twin loads ripped up through Jody Butler's skull, tearing his flesh and bone to shreds and spraying blood and brains across the street. Bright spouts of blood jetted up from the lacerated stump where his head had been. Jody's corpse rocked back in the saddle as his horse jerked aside, the reins slipping through Bodie's fingers.

There was a long moment of stunned silence, every figure on the street seeming to come to a dead stop. Bodie twisted round, his gaze raking the men on the boardwalk, and his right hand was already dragging his Colt from its holster.

On the edge of the boardwalk, his face pale with shock at the result of his actions, stood Frank Lowery. His revolver was in his raised right hand, powdersmoke still curling from the muzzle. His momentary shock, holding him rigid, delayed any further action he might have been contemplating.

Bodie didn't allow him any time to recover. He snapped the barrel of the Colt down at Lowery's body and triggered off a shot. The bullet ripped into Lowery's soft stomach, blasting a pulpy hole in the small of his back on its way out. Blood began to boil from the wound, staining the front of Lowery's pants. He lurched back across the boardwalk, his mouth sagging in pained surprise. Bodie's second shot ripped through the left side of his face, baring white bone and glistening flesh and the third bullet caved in his nose before driving through his skull. Lowery flopped on to the dirty boardwalk, his loose body jerking about in his death throes, blood streaming from the gaping wounds in his flesh, spattering across the worn planks in bright runnels.

The second he'd triggered the third shot Bodie leaned forward over his horse's neck and drove his heels in hard. The animal bolted across the street, dust spuming up behind him. Bodie knew that he had no more than seconds before every gun on that boardwalk opened up on him, and he wanted to have at least a small chance. He jammed his Colt back in its holster and yanked the Winchester from its scabbard — and that was the moment when the guns opened up. He felt the horse shudder, was aware of the solid thwack of bullets driving into its flesh. The animal screamed, twisted sideways and began to go down. Bodie kicked his feet from the stirrups and left the saddle in a frantic dive. He hit the street on his face, scrambling wildly to his feet, and, forgoing his dignity, ran for his life . . .

14

BULLETS chewed ragged splinters from the verandah posts and the boardwalk itself as Bodie gained the scant protection of the covered way. He was far from any alley he might use and staying where he was could only get him killed. The only direction left open to him was forward — and that was the way Bodie went.

His desperate lunge took him head first through the wide display window of a men's outfitters. Bodie curled his body into a ball and went with his momentum. He scattered bolts of cloth and metal stands set out in the window, crashing through the flimsy partition blocking off the windows from the main part of the store. Bodie grunted as he hit the floor beyond, uncurling his body and coming to his feet in a shower of broken glass.

He found himself confronted by the owner of the store; a balding, thin, small man who stared at Bodie in horror. His startled eyes bulged behind the thick lens of his steel-rimmed glasses and his naturally pale face turned a sickly white. The store owner found himself shocked into speechlessness and all he could do was to stare up at the towering figure of the grim-faced, battered and bloody man who had literally exploded into his life.

Bodie had no time for such dalliance. He knew that he had done no more than gain himself a few moments — a brief chance to at least prepare himself for the trouble that was bound to come. With Jody dead — accident or not — Howard Butler had his excuse for whatever followed and he was liable to have Elkhorn torn apart plank by plank to get his hands on Bodie.

He pushed by the paralysed store owner and made for the rear of the gloomy building, kicking open a door that opened on to a cluttered workroom. There was another on the far side of the room and this led to the store's backlot.

As Bodie stepped into the hard glare of the sunlight he heard a sudden commotion from the front of the store — and guessed that his free time was almost up.

His keyed-up senses, alert for the slightest indication of danger, meant that he was more than ready for the sudden appearance of an armed man rounding the end of a building ahead of him.

The man had a rifle in his hands. His face creased into a savage grin as he spotted Bodie, and he was congratulating himself on being the first to make contact with the manhunter, when Bodie swung his Winchester round and pumped two bullets into his body. The man felt the solid smack of the bullets as they drove deep into his chest. The force of the bullets shoved him backwards, off his feet, and as he went down he became aware of the rising pain in his body. He had never been shot before, so there was no way he could anticipate the effect the bullets were going to have on him. All he could understand was the initial burst of pain and then the terrible numbness, the terror that rose as he realised that he couldn't breathe properly. And when he choked on something filling his throat he coughed out a frothy gout of blood. He slipped over on to his back and lay staring up at the wide blue sky, wondering why there was such a deep silence all around him. Even then he wasn't aware that he was dying . . .

Bodie ran on, passing the fallen man. He glanced down the alley and saw shadowed, running figures pounding towards him. He twisted round to face them, triggering swift shots the length of the narrow alley, and the men were unable to avoid the blistering hail of lead that tore at their flesh, spattering thick gouts of their blood on the faded boards of the buildings around them.

Only one of them had time for a shot, the bullet exploding dry wood dust into Bodie's face. The manhunter levered a fresh round into the Winchester's breech, inclined the muzzle and put a bullet through the head of his attacker. There was a sudden thud as the man's head was rapped against the side of the building by the slam of the bullet. His mouth flew open and then the back of his skull exploded outwards, shedding a greasy spray of blood, bone and brains that clung thickly to the side of the building.

The street was out of the question Bodie realised. Butler's men would be in every alley, all of them eventually reaching the backlot. Bodie turned and moved away from the town, making for the thick, tangled brush and the tall timber that formed a natural windbreak behind the town. Even as he started his long run he knew he wasn't going to make it without being spotted.

The first bullets started to whack a ragged line across the ground, moving closer and closer to Bodie as he ran on. He began to feel the wind of their passing, the hiss of dry earth slapping his pants as bullets kicked up thick geysers. He didn't bother to return their fire. That would be just stupid. The kind of move to get him well and truly killed. He could trade shots with them when he was in some kind of protective position. He began to duck and weave, doing his best to make himself a difficult target for the exploring guns.

He burst into the thick brush to the accompaniment of bullets that ripped at the green leaves, shredding bark from the trees. He stumbled once on a knotted root, and as he struggled to his feet, chest heaving from his exertions, he heard the thud of horses' hooves drumming over the hard ground.

Bodie saw them as they neared the timber, their dark shapes large and menacing as they were outlined against the bright sunlight. He jerked his rifle to his shoulder and triggered shot after shot in their direction. He heard a horse squeal in pain, saw it rear back, spilling its rider from the saddle. The rider gave a startled yell as he hit the ground, and then the yell turned to a scream as Bodie put a bullet into the moving figure. The man lurched to his feet, crashing through the brush.

Angry voices called out to each other. They cursed Bodie and they cursed each other. There was rage and fear and confusion in the voices. Guns were fired, adding their noise to the din.

Bodie pushed his way through the timber. He lurched forward, chest high in tangled brush, and felt the ground suddenly slope away from him. There was no chance of turning back. He slithered down the long slope, rolling the last few yards and felt the sudden shock of cold water as he came to rest in the swift running stream that cut its way through this part of the forest. Bodie dragged himself to his feet. He scooped up a handful of water and splashed his grimy face.

The chill of the water cleared some of the muzziness from his head. When Bodie reached down to scoop up more water he saw that his hand was streaked with red. Only then did he begin to feel the bites of pain from the gashes and the lacerations in his flesh. He recalled his impulsive dive through the store window and figured he was lucky to have come away from it with only a few cuts.

That luck was fast running out, he decided, as he splashed his way across to the far bank of the stream. He heard brush crackling above him. A horse edged through the brittle tangle of greenery at the top of the slope. The rider was peering down in the direction of the stream, obviously able to see the marks Bodie had made during his descent of the slope. It would only be seconds before his eyes located Bodie.

The Winchester swung up, butt nestling against Bodie's shoulder. He eased back on the trigger. The Winchester blasted a gout of flame and the rider jerked in his saddle as the bullet tore in under his ribs, angling up through his body and then penetrated his heart. Blood fountained out across the greenery, dappling the leaves, soaking quickly into the soft earth. The rider slumped to the side, falling from his horse almost gracefully. He arced out over the slope, landing on his face halfway down, and rolled loosely to the bottom. For a moment his body held itself on the very edge of the stream, then it slid gently into the water and the clear flow turned a cloudy red, then pink as the blood was diluted.

The horse stayed where it was, only glancing round once as it realised that its rider had gone.

Bodie recrossed the stream and climbed the slope, hoping that the animal stayed where it was long enough for him to reach it. It did. And it remained passive as Bodie picked up the trailing reins and swung himself into the saddle. He took up the slack and prodded the horse into movement. The animal responded without hesitation. Bodie cut along the crest of the slope, then tightened the reins and brought the horse to a dead stop as he spotted riders moving through the trees ahead of him.

He searched the timber in every direction, waiting, just biding his time. When he saw a gap, over to his right, he eased the horse's head round in that direction and worked his way through the trees. Again he stopped. He looked and he listened. A weary smile touched his lips. The riders were all behind him. And they were moving further away all the time. Bodie chuckled softly. The damn fools were bunched together like sheep instead of spreading out to cover more ground.

Bodie rode out of the timber and looked down on Elkhorn. The town looked peaceful enough. But there would be Butler men still on the streets. Bodie touched his heels to the horse's sides. If he had his way there would be dead Butler men on the streets very soon.

He circled the town and came in from the north end. As he moved towards the rutted trail that would eventually become the main street he saw a bunch of horsemen drift out of the shadows of the high livery stable. Bodie swore, snatching his Winchester up off his hip, the barrel lining up on the riders.

And then he relaxed, the rifle sagging, relief washing over him in a welcome flood.

The lead rider was Amos Skellhorn!

15

"BODIE, you've got more damn lives than a dozen cats!" Skellhorn said, genuine pleasure in his voice.

"One of the requirements in my line of work," Bodie replied. He ran his eyes over the bunch of grim, heavily-armed men flanking Skellhorn. "You work some kind of medicine to conjure this bunch up?"

Skellhorn grinned. "Every man here is from the Kittyhawk. When Butler dragged me to town and told me he was holding Fran I got damned angry. So before I come after you I cut back to the Kittyhawk and gathered the boys together. I figured we could play sneaky, too. The boys just hung around town waiting for me to get back. They kept out of sight until they were needed. That time's been a fair piece comin' — but she's here now, Bodie, and one way or another we're havin' us a reckoning here in Elkhorn. Time we settled with the Major and his crew for all those years they've pushed us around. We want Elkhorn to be our town. A place where every man can come and go where he pleases, when he pleases. And then we can forget we ever had to call it Hangtown!"

"Butler isn't likely to step down without a fight," Bodie said. "A lot of men could die here today — on both sides."

"That ain't stoppin' you!" Skellhorn pointed out.

Bodie grinned. "I got my reasons," he said. "Mainly they're financial and some are just out and out meanness."

"Comes right down to it, Bodie, money is at the back of it all. The Major figures him having so much of it makes it right to do what he likes with other folks' lives. And I just can't abide bein' thought of as a man who'll throw away his life's work for a handful of dollar bills!"

"Anybody got any spare shells for my Winchester?" Bodie asked. He was handed a fresh box of cartridges by one of the Kittyhawk riders. Bodie reloaded the rifle and returned the box to the man.

"Let's go," Amos Skellhorn said softly.

They spread out as they moved down the street, horses plodding steadily along the dust strip. Rifle barrels glinted dully in the blazing heat. Dust rose in a thin, pale cloud, misting the hot air.

The gaol lay before them, seemingly deserted. In fact the whole of Elkhorn presented a silent image to the advancing Kittyhawk riders.

But there was an unreal mood hanging over the town. A false sense of calm. Which was abruptly shattered by the sharp crack of a single gunshot.

A Kittyhawk rider slumped forward in his saddle, blood pouring from a wound in his arm.

White powdersmoke drifted from the half open door of the gaol.

"Take'em," Amos Skellhorn ordered.

There was a brief, heavy silence — and then the street echoed to the thunderous racket of concentrated gunfire. The front of the jail became hazed with dust as bullets hammered splinters from the hewn stone. The heavy door splintered, wood slivers filling the air. The glass windows fronting the jail were shattered, even the wooden frames chewed apart by the unceasing barrage of lead.

"Butler! Butler, get out here!" Amos Skellhorn yelled. "Step out or we'll burn you out!"

"Hell, Amos, we came to do, not to talk!" one of the Kittyhawk men said. "Let's just get on with it!"

"Yeah!" agreed another. "Time for talkin' is over!"

He turned to fire at the jail again. As he did a rifle blasted from the jail. The bullet hit the man directly between the eyes, caving in the front of his face. Flesh disappeared in a gush of thick blood. The man twisted from his saddle and thudded limply to the street. The back of his skull glistened with red where the bullet had split his skull.

"Sam! Sam!" Amos Skellhorn roared.

"Here!" A thick set man with a red face guided his horse close to Skellhorn's.

"Get that damn oil!" Skellhorn yelled above the gunfire. "Toss it inside the jail! We'll burn the bastards out!"

The bunched Kittyhawk riders began to break apart as more guns opened up from inside the jail.

Bodie, who had stayed on the flank of the attack, was the first to spot the riders sweeping in along the street. They were the men Butler had sent after him. The ones he'd avoided and left up in the timber. The shooting had drawn them back to Elkhorn.

The Butler men opened fire. One Kittyhawk rider went down as his horse was hit. The rider scrambled to his feet, then made the mistake of going back to pick up the rifle he'd dropped. He had only just closed his fingers over the weapon when the bunch of Butler men reached him. There was a short-lived scream as the man vanished beneath the pounding hooves. When the riders had passed and the dust cleared the body could be seen lying in the dust. The horses had trampled him into the earth, pulping his flesh and splintering bones. Blood glistened wetly on the torn flesh, the white shards of splintered bone.

Bodie had reined his horse to the far side of the street as the riders drove on by. He put his rifle to his shoulder and shot two of the riders off their horses. One landed face down, skidding along the street for yards before he came to rest, dead, against a horse trough. The other landed on his side, twisting frantically, right hand at his side, fingers clawing at the gun he wore on his hip. Bodie's bullet had gouged a raw wound across his side and blood was pouring from the tear in the side of his shirt. Despite the wound the rider made a deliberate attempt to get his gun out. Bodie shot him through the chest, the Winchester's bullet jerking him halfway to his feet and hurling him up on to the boardwalk where he lay spouting blood all over the worn planking.

The street had become an arena of shooting, shouting, dying, screaming, desperate men. They all had one thing in common: none of them wanted to die — none of them wanted to be hurt — but a lot of them were getting hurt and a number of them were dying. But there was no way anyone could have stopped the slaughter. There was too much emotion and frustration being used as a driving force. Pent up rage was being expelled in one violent surge, and sense and reason had no place on that bloody street.

The front of the jail suddenly blossomed with flames. A great sheet of orange, writhing and curling, swelled up and out. The heat could be felt halfway across the street. A great pall of black, greasy smoke hung over the jail. The door burst open and cringing figures ran out of the jail. Some had their clothing alight and they rolled in the dust of the street, trying to put out the flames. As one of them succeeded he staggered to his feet, only to be cut down by the combined power of three rifles fired in unison. Bright blood contrasted with the soot-blackened clothing the man was wearing.

As the two sides began to drift apart, seeking cover, the street began to empty — save for the dead and dying. Bodie, abandoning his skittish horse, spotted a figure slipping away from the side of the jail. There was something very familiar about the man.

Bodie took a longer look.

It was Lee Haddon.

Tossing aside his rifle Bodie went after him, loosening the heavy Colt in its holster. Haddon was already way down the street, keeping to the shadowed boardwalks. It didn't take Bodie long to figure out Haddon's destination.

The livery stable.

And he was right.

He caught up with Haddon just as the man reached the stable doors.

"Haddon!" Bodie called.

Lee Haddon paused, turned slowly, his eyes glinting coldly as he faced Bodie. He stood relaxed, hands at his sides, but Bodie knew that deep inside Lee Haddon was primed and ready to move.

"Bodie, you're gettin' to be a pain in the ass!" Haddon said. "I figured you'd be long gone by now!"

"Never leave a job unfinished," Bodie said.

Haddon grinned. "An' you left me 'til last!" His mood changed suddenly. "But you won't find me as easy as Jody! I ain't no pissant, bounty hunter!"

"I'll just ask you one thing, Haddon," Bodie said.

"Yeah?"

"You comin' back to Pine Ridge with me? Sitting a saddle? Or are we doin' it the hard way?"

Lee Haddon shook his head. "I ain't goin' back to Pine Ridge, Bodie, sittin', standin', or lying!"

Bodie's question was answered. He didn't see the point in pursuing the matter further. Talk wasn't going to get him Lee Haddon. That left one way out.

Lee Haddon saw the manhunter reach for his gun, and he grinned. It was obvious that Bodie wasn't aware of Haddon's skill with a handgun. His fast draw and the fact that he seldom missed what he was aiming at. That might have been true that day in Elkhorn, but Lee Haddon didn't have the chance to find out. Bodie's Colt hammered out its shots in rapid order. Haddon figured there had to be something wrong. He'd barely started to lift his weapon. Then Bodie's bullets caught him in the chest, cleaving through flesh and muscle, breaking bones. One bullet emerged between his shoulders, bits of lung gouting out of the pulpy hole along with a lot of blood. Haddon felt himself turned around by the bullets. He smacked face first against the stable door, and tried to keep himself on his feet by hanging on to the door. Not that it was any good. His fingers refused to grip and his legs weakened. Haddon slid to the ground. He lay and watched Bodie approach. The manhunter was still carrying his gun. He stood over Haddon, the muzzle of the big gun aimed at Haddon's head. A loud blast of sound filled Haddon's skull. The world exploded into brilliant light that grew and grew, the brightness becoming so intense that it finally burst and a soothing darkness rolled over him. It enveloped him completely, blotting out sound and heat, and it was so comfortable that Haddon decided he wouldn't even try resisting.

Bodie flipped open the loading gate of his Colt and took out the empty casings. He thumbed in fresh loads, and turned away from Lee Haddon's bloody corpse.

The gunfire had slackened considerably. Riderless horses drifted along the street. Here and there wounded men moved aimlessly about, seemingly unaware of their surroundings.

Bodie walked up the street, blinking his eyes against the drifting smoke still pouring from the jail. He spotted a figure coming towards him and lifted the Colt, but the figure limped forward, raising a hand. It was Amos Skellhorn. He had a bloody wound in his left thigh.

"You get him?" he asked. "Haddon?"

Bodie nodded. "That only leaves Butler!"

Skellhorn shook his head. "You're too late, Bodie!"

He led Bodie to where a group of Kittyhawk men were gathered round a crumpled shape lying in the dust in front of the jail. What was left of the Major — Howard Butler — lay in a congealing pool of his own blood. He'd been literally shot to pieces. Every Kittyhawk gun must have been turned on him, countless bullets ripping him open from skull to groin. Great raw, pulped wounds showed where shots had been put in him from close range, tearing out chunks of living flesh. His shredded clothing was sodden with blood and it was caked around his open mouth. Butler's lips were drawn back in a final snarl of defiance. In death he looked far older than he had in life. Smaller, too, as he lay curled up in the dirt — as if he had rolled up his body in a futile, almost childlike attempt to escape the final punishment.

"He came out ready to take us all on," Skellhorn said. "The son of a bitch had a gun in each hand. Shooting at every damn thing in sight. He killed one of our boys before we stopped him. He'd've killed us all, Bodie."

"You put his back to the wall," Bodie said. "He was an old wolf,

Skellhorn. And that's when an old wolf fights the best — when he's got his back to the wall!"

Skellhorn shook his head. When he looked up there was a glint in his eyes "Us sheep didn't do too bad for once," he said. "The Major wasn't the only one with his back to the wall. Even sheep get tired of bein' carved up..."

Thick smoke rolled across the street, sending men running, coughing, eyes streaming.

"You going to ride back to Pine Ridge?" Skellhorn asked. "Collect that bounty?"

Bodie nodded. "Damn right I am. Ain't had to work so hard for a long time!"

"You ain't in all that much of a hurry to leave are you?" Skellhorn probed. "Nothing to stop you sending a telegraph to Pine Ridge — tellin' 'em you got what you came for!"

"You asking me to stay?"

"He might not — but I will!"

Bodie turned and it was Fran. She was looking at him with that expression women were prone to showing when they were past playing games. Bodie knew that look too damn well. He'd seen it so often it was like being greeted by an old friend — yet at the same time he knew it could mean trouble. He gazed at Fran for a long moment, caught the slow smile curling the corners of her soft mouth, and he thought what the hell! A man has a right to a few quiet moments, and with a girl like Fran there was no chance of getting bored. And he couldn't get himself in any worse trouble than the mess he'd just been through.

Could he?

He took Fran's arm and let her lead him across the street towards the restaurant, and ignored the persistent small voice at the back of his mind. The voice that kept telling him he could! He already knew that — but he was damned if he was going to allow it to spoil his fun!